"Do you guys rea~~lly think that everything hap~~pens for a reason?" ~~really some big plan~~ ~~bits and pieces, or~~ ~~because it makes th~~

"I don't think yo~~u can look at~~ Cooper told her. "One thing leads into another, but it's not like we're all just acting out some big play that somebody else wrote."

"How do you know that for sure?" asked Annie. "We can think anything we want to, but how do we know? How do we know our lives aren't already planned out for us?"

"By who?" Kate asked her.

Annie shrugged. "I don't know. The Fates. The Goddess. Whoever."

"I don't buy that," Cooper said. "I think we're given a path to walk, but I think that path has lots of different side paths. We choose the ones we want to go down."

"Maybe," Annie said.

circle of three

BOOK
12

written in the stars

isobel bird

AVON BOOKS

An Imprint of HarperCollinsPublishers

Library of Congress Catalog Card Number: 2001118052
ISBN 0-06-000604-8

First Avon edition, 2001

❖

AVON TRADEMARK REG. U.S. PAT. OFF. AND IN OTHER COUNTRIES,
MARCA REGISTRADA, HECHO EN U.S.A.

Visit us on the World Wide Web!
www.harperteen.com

CHAPTER 1

"Ten!"
"Nine!"
"Eight!"
"Seven!"
"Six!"
"Five!"
"Four!"
"Three!"
"Two!"
"One!"
"Happy New Year!"

A shower of brightly colored confetti rained down from overhead as Annie looked around at the happy, smiling faces of her friends. The noise of horns and laughter filled her ears, and all around her people were hugging and kissing each other in celebration of the new year. She turned, looking for someone to celebrate with, and saw Tyler standing behind her. *Why not?* she thought after hesitating for a moment. She opened her arms.

"Happy New Year," she said, stepping toward him.

She bumped into Kate, who had stepped forward at exactly the same moment. The two of them stopped and looked at one another awkwardly. Annie glanced at Tyler and saw that he was looking uncomfortably at the floor.

"Happy New Year," Annie said, trying to sound enthusiastic, and put her arms around Kate.

Kate hugged her back. "Happy New Year," she said softly.

The two friends parted and stood next to one another, not saying anything. Tyler had disappeared into the crowd. Annie wished she could do the same thing. What had she been thinking? She should have known that something like this would happen. It was hard enough being at the party with both Tyler and Kate there; even *thinking* about giving him a celebratory kiss should have been off-limits. It had only been a little more than a month since Kate had found out about the brief sort-of-affair between Annie and Tyler, and things between them were still slightly tense.

"Hey, you guys, what's with the gloomy expressions?" Cooper and Sasha came up to Annie and Kate. Cooper had dyed her hair bright red for the occasion. Seeing it for the first time earlier in the evening, Annie had remarked that she looked like a living sparkler.

"I think they need some sweeties to kiss," Sasha

said, grinning. She looked at Cooper. "Shall we save them from their misery?"

"By all means," Cooper replied. She turned and kissed Annie as Sasha planted one on Kate. "Happy New Year!"

Annie and Kate couldn't help but laugh. Their friends' silliness had broken the tension. The four of them stood together, surrounded by the noise of the party. They were at Thea's house, where their classmates and teachers from their weekly Wicca study group had gathered—along with the members of the Coven of the Green Wood and assorted friends—to ring in the new year. They had spent the past few hours eating and talking, waiting for the big moment to arrive. Now that it had, the party seemed to really get going. Someone turned on music, and people began dancing.

"Let's go out on the porch," Sasha said over the music. "It's getting crowded in here and I'm hot."

The four friends wove their way through the dancers, escaping into the kitchen and then out onto the deck at the back of the house. Annie, the last one to leave, shut the door behind her, blocking out the sound of the music. The girls collapsed into chairs on the porch.

"I never thought I'd be the one to need a break from a party," remarked Cooper, laughing. "Those witches sure can get rowdy."

"I know," added Sasha. "Give them a little more

of my mom's punch and they'll be doing a circle dance all over the place."

They sat quietly for a while, looking up at the night sky. The moon was halfway to fullness, and the winter sky looked like black ice embedded with diamonds. The air was cold, but there was no wind, and the coolness felt good on their warm skin.

"So, who made resolutions?" Sasha asked after a few minutes. She looked around questioningly at the others.

"I don't make resolutions," Cooper said. "It just sets me up for failure, and who needs that?"

"Oh, come on," Sasha shot back. "I know you. You'd never turn down a challenge. Spill it. What have you resolved to change this year? No, let me guess. You're going to volunteer at a soup kitchen, stop swearing, and lay off chocolate."

Cooper snorted. "Yeah," she said. "Right after I save the rain forests and learn French. Hardly."

"Then, what *are* you going to do?" Kate asked her.

Cooper shook her head, looking annoyed. "You're not supposed to tell anyone your resolutions," she said. "That way no one else knows when you break them ten minutes later."

"We'll tell you ours if you tell us yours," Annie teased.

Cooper sighed. "Fine," she said. "If you really want to know, I have three resolutions."

"Three?" Sasha said, sounding shocked. "Aren't you ambitious."

"And not one of them is laying off chocolate," Cooper informed her. She looked around at her friends. "I can't believe I'm telling you guys this. Okay, the first one is that I'm going to try to get along better with my mother."

"That's a good one," said Annie. "Very classic."

"Yeah, well, it's probably the hardest one," said Cooper. "She's been a real pain since my dad moved out. Anyway, the second one is about my music. I want to write a bunch of songs with Jane and actually record a CD."

"Impressive," Kate remarked. "Does Jane know about this plan?"

"Not yet," Cooper answered. "My dad said he'd help us out. One of his clients owns a recording studio, and he owes my dad a favor. Now I just have to convince Jane to do it."

"How hard can that be?" Sasha asked. "I'd think she'd be all over that."

Cooper nodded. "I hope she will be," she said. "You never know with Jane."

"Where is she tonight, anyway?" said Kate. "I thought you invited her."

"I did," replied Cooper. "She said she had another party to go to."

"Okay, so far we have being nice to Mom and becoming a rock star," said Sasha. "What's number three?"

"That's the easiest one," Cooper said. "I want to lose ten pounds so I look better in a swimsuit."

The other three stared at her, their mouths open in surprise. Cooper looked back at them for a moment, then smiled. "Got you," she said.

The others groaned. "You had us there for a second," Annie said. "I was waiting for you to tell us that you were going to have a boob job, too."

"That's *next* year," Cooper quipped. "Seriously, though, my third resolution is to exercise a little more. I know it's boring, but it would be nice to actually move around a little every now and again. Not *too* much. But maybe a little running or swimming or something."

"I'm impressed," Kate said. "Your resolutions are much better than mine."

"Which are?" asked Cooper.

Kate took a deep breath. "Actually, there's just one."

"It better be a good one, then," Sasha said. "There's no grading on a curve when it comes to resolutions, you know."

"It's pretty big," Kate said. "I've decided that this year I'm going to be totally honest."

Cooper groaned. "Oh, please," she said. "When's the last time you told a lie?"

"That's not really what I mean," said Kate. "I mean I'm going to be honest about what I want. I'm tired of doing what other people want me to do or expect me to do. I'm tired of pretending to be something I'm not just so my family will be happier. So from now on I'm going to tell the truth, even when it's hard."

"I take it back," Cooper said. "That's major. Good for you."

"Thanks," Kate said. "But I might need you guys to remind me every so often that I promised to do this."

"Don't worry," Annie told her. "That's our job."

"What about you, Ms. Crandall?" Cooper said. "What's on your to-do list for the year?"

"Mine seems really dull compared to yours," answered Annie. "I kind of went the traditional route."

"As in not-biting-your-nails traditional?" Kate asked.

Annie nodded. "Sort of," she said. "I want to spend more time painting, and I want to learn how to do something cool."

"I *knew* someone was going to learn French," Cooper said. "Thank Goddess it isn't me."

"Not like that," Annie said. "I mean something to do with witchcraft. You know, like working with herbs or drumming or something. I haven't really decided yet."

"Anything else?" asked Sasha.

"Not unless you count achieving world peace," Annie said seriously.

"I don't," answered Sasha. "Okay. My turn."

"She's been waiting for this all night," Cooper remarked to the others. "I bet she even has a list written out."

"As a matter of fact, I do," Sasha said. She fished

in the pocket of her shirt and pulled out a folded piece of paper. Opening it, she cleared her throat. "Number one," she said. "I hereby resolve to commit to a year and a day of studying Wicca, so that next year we'll *all* be real witches."

"You're assuming that the three of us are going to *be* real witches," Kate said.

"Whatever," answered Sasha, waving her hand at Kate. "Number two. I hereby resolve to do better in school so that my mother stops worrying that I'll be left back and end up the oldest sophomore at Beecher Falls High School."

The others laughed, although they knew that Sasha was only half kidding. Sasha glared at them, pretending to be annoyed, and they stopped.

"Number three," she read. "I hereby resolve to do daily meditation for at least ten minutes. Number four. I hereby resolve not to think about kissing Fred Durst more than five times while doing daily meditation."

"Fred Durst!" Cooper exclaimed. "Can't you do any better than that?"

Sasha put down her list of resolutions. "And number five," she said firmly, looking directly at Cooper. "I hereby resolve not to let the faults of others irritate me."

"It does not say that," Cooper retorted. "Give me that paper."

Sasha stuffed the paper back into her pocket. "Okay, so that one I made up off the top of my head," she said. "But I think it's a good one, so I'm officially adding it."

"Sorry," Cooper said. "All resolutions must be submitted before midnight or they're null and void. I'm afraid you'll have to stick with better grades and not fantasizing about playing kissy face with Limp Bizkit boy."

"Ten bucks says I can go without Fred longer than you can be nice to your mother," replied Sasha.

"Twenty," Cooper said. "And you're on."

The two of them shook hands. Annie looked at Kate. "I don't think they're good influences on us," she said.

"No," agreed Kate. "They're very bad. I think we should stop talking to them."

"Go right ahead," Sasha said. "But your parties will be really dull without us around."

"Not to mention your full moon circles," Cooper added.

Everyone laughed some more, then they grew quiet again as each sat with her own thoughts, listening to the sounds of the party inside. A few minutes later the back door opened and three more people came out onto the deck. One of them was Archer, who the girls knew from their class at Crones' Circle bookstore. Another was Jace Myers, who they also knew slightly. She was a rabbi, as well as a psychic, and the girls had met her in October when they'd taken Annie to Jace's house for a birthday reading. They had never met the third woman before.

"Hey there," Archer said. "What are you four up to?"

"Just enjoying the quiet," said Kate. "It was getting a little bit crowded in there."

"Tell me about it," Jace commented. "I think there are fewer people in Times Square than at this party." Jace turned to Annie. "How did things work out with your ghosts?" she asked, referring to the reading she'd done for Annie on her birthday, in which the spirits of Annie's deceased parents had spoken to her.

"Oh, it was all fine," Annie answered. "Weird, but fine."

Jace nodded. "I thought it would be," she said.

Annie looked up at the night sky. Seeing Jace brought back all the memories of the period when she'd thought that her parents' ghosts were angry at her. She'd even gone back to their old house in San Francisco and attempted a ritual to send them back to the spirit realm. Luckily, she'd figured out what was really happening and had been able to speak with her parents on the night of Samhain. Doing that had helped heal the hurt she'd been carrying around inside of her since their deaths, and she'd finally been able to move on with her life.

Even better, while in San Francisco she had met Becka Dunning and her father, Grayson, who now lived in the house where Annie and her family had lived. Annie and Becka had become friends. Mr. Dunning and Annie's Aunt Sarah had also hit it off, and had been seeing a lot of each other since October. In fact, Annie's aunt was on a weekend trip with Grayson Dunning at that very moment. She was due to come home the following afternoon, and Annie couldn't wait to hear how things had gone.

"The stars are so bright tonight," Annie remarked. "Look at that one just below the moon. It's like someone turned on its high beams or something."

"That's not a star," said the woman who had come out with Jace and Archer. "It's a planet. Jupiter, actually."

"Everyone, this is Olivia Sorensen," Archer said as the others looked at the woman. "She's going to be teaching class for the next couple of weeks as we study astrology."

"You're an astrologer?" Kate asked.

"And an astronomer," Olivia answered. "I work for the planetarium. A number of years ago I was asked to write a paper debunking astrology. Unfortunately for the journal that asked me to write the paper, I became a believer instead. Now I do both."

"Olivia is amazing," Archer told the girls. "I have her do my chart every year, and she always surprises me with how on target she is."

"Well, it *is* a science," Olivia said. "Although I admit that it takes different skills to read an astrological chart correctly. You have to be willing to go beyond the realm of numbers and formulas and see the larger pattern they're a part of."

Annie studied the woman carefully. She herself had a scientific mind, and she was always interested in meeting others who, like her, were involved in things that traditional scientists might consider a little too weird. Olivia definitely looked like a science person. Her blond hair was cut shoulder length, and she was dressed in black pants and a dark blue shirt. Also, she wore glasses with black plastic frames, much like the ones Annie herself wore. As Annie watched, Olivia reached up and pushed the glasses up her nose in a familiar gesture that made Annie smile to herself. *She's a lot like me,* she thought. *I'm going to like her.*

"Are you a witch?" Sasha asked Olivia.

"Me?" Olivia said, sounding surprised and a little embarrassed. "Sort of. I mean, I'm not *officially* a witch or anything. I don't belong to a coven. But I'm interested in Wicca." She paused for a moment. "I guess you could say that I'm witch lite."

Annie laughed. Olivia glanced at her and smiled shyly, then laughed, too, as if sharing a private joke. The others looked at them in mild amusement. Then Cooper looked at her watch.

"It's almost time for me to be in bed," she said, standing up. "Who wants a ride home?"

"I do," Annie said.

"Kate?" asked Cooper.

"Sure," said Kate. "Let me get my coat."

The girls stood up to say good-bye to their friends. "I guess we'll see you on Tuesday," Annie said to Olivia as they shook hands.

"I'm looking forward to it," Olivia replied.

Kate, Cooper, and Annie went inside, leaving Sasha and the others on the deck. They collected their coats, said good-bye to a few more friends, and left. Soon they were in Cooper's car on the way home.

Cooper dropped Kate off first, then headed to Annie's.

"I noticed the two of you pretty much stayed away from Tyler all evening," Cooper said. "Any news there?"

"No," Annie said. "We don't talk about it. I kind of wish we could, because right now it just feels like this big thing standing between us. I can't even imagine how Tyler feels about it."

"It will work itself out," Cooper told her. "You and Kate have been through too much together. We all have. You just need to give it time."

"I know," Annie said. "But it makes me sad."

As they pulled up to the Crandall house, they saw that there was an unfamiliar car parked in the driveway. Also, there were lights on in the house.

"That's weird," Annie said. "Meg is staying at her friend Amy's house tonight. Aunt Sarah isn't supposed to be home until tomorrow."

Suddenly she was filled with an overwhelming fear. Something was wrong. Something bad had happened. As soon as Cooper stopped the car, Annie got out and ran to the front door. Fumbling with her key, she unlocked the door and ran inside. There she found her aunt standing in the living room. Grayson Dunning was with her.

"Perfect timing," Aunt Sarah said as Annie stared at them. "We just got here."

"You're not supposed to be back until tomorrow," Annie said, confused.

"I know," her aunt said. "But we wanted to come home and tell you."

"Tell me what?" Annie asked. "What's wrong?"

"Nothing's wrong," Mr. Dunning said.

"Not at all," added Annie's aunt. "In fact, everything is great." She looked at Mr. Dunning and smiled. Then she looked at Annie. "Grayson and I are getting married," she said.

CHAPTER 2

"How was your party?"

Cooper was seated on a chair the next day, facing Jane's bed. Jane was sitting on the bed, propped up against a pile of pillows. Her guitar was resting on her lap, and she was halfheartedly strumming it. She seemed distracted, and Cooper was trying to figure out what was wrong.

"What?" Jane said, looking up as if she'd forgotten that Cooper was in the room. Her long black hair hung down in her face, and she didn't make any move to push it out of her eyes.

"I was just asking how your party was last night," Cooper repeated.

"Oh," said Jane. "It was okay, I guess." She went back to playing her guitar without saying anything else.

Cooper put down her guitar. "Okay," she said. "What gives? Where's the endearingly bitter Jane I know and love?"

Jane stopped playing. "I'm just tired," she said. "It was a long night."

Cooper eyed her suspiciously. "There's something else," she said. "I can tell. Are you pissed that your family isn't here?"

Jane's parents were frequently away on business. In fact, Cooper had yet to meet them, as they'd always been gone on some trip whenever she came over to the Goldstein house. Similarly, Jane's two older sisters were both away at college, and Cooper had only seen pictures of them. The only member of Jane's family she'd ever met was her grandfather. A survivor of the Holocaust, he was a quiet man who frequently seemed not to know where he was or what was going on. But on more than one occasion he'd shown himself to be almost psychic in his understanding of people and their problems, and Cooper had come to really care about the old man. She knew that Jane did, too, although Cooper suspected that having to care for her grandfather so often was probably very hard on her friend.

"No," Jane said. "This isn't about them. I'm used to them being gone."

She stopped, not saying anything else. Cooper waited impatiently. She wanted Jane to tell her what was wrong, but she knew that pushing her would only make her retreat farther into herself. Instead, Cooper picked out a soft melody on her guitar, tempering the deep silence in the room with the sound of her playing.

"Have you ever broken up with someone?" Jane asked suddenly.

Cooper shook her head. "I've only ever gone out with one guy," she answered. "T.J. I've *almost* broken up with him about a dozen times, though. Does that count?"

Jane smiled weakly. "Afraid not," she said. "But thanks anyway."

"Is that what happened?" asked Cooper.

Jane nodded. "Last night," she said. "Great timing, huh?"

Cooper was confused. "How could you break up with someone?" she said. "I didn't even know you were *seeing* someone."

Jane shrugged. "What can I say?" she replied. "I'm a woman of mystery."

"That you are," said Cooper. "So tell me everything. What was the jerk's name?"

"It doesn't matter," Jane said. "It wasn't anyone important."

"It must have been someone at least a little important for you to be getting all gloomy about it," answered Cooper. "I've never seen you even look at a guy before, and here you've been dating one. How long had you been going out, anyway?"

"A while," said Jane vaguely. "I guess it was a big deal because this was kind of my first real relationship, too. You know, like with you and T.J."

"And he dumped you on New Year's Eve?" Cooper said. "What kind of creep would do that?"

"I know it's stupid," said Jane. "I mean, no one expects high school romances to last, right?" She looked at Cooper, then added, "I'm sorry. I didn't mean that you and T.J.—"

"It's okay," Cooper said. "Don't think I haven't thought about that myself. You're right. People change. They go off to college and grow apart and all of that stuff. It's one of the reasons I was hesitant about getting involved with T.J. in the first place."

"Then why did you?" Jane asked.

Cooper smiled. "Believe it or not, my mother talked me into it," she said. "She said that I should think of dating in high school as practice for real life."

"If real life is anything like high school, I'm on the next bus out of here," Jane said, throwing herself back against the pillows.

"I don't really like that image either," admitted Cooper. "But the more I thought about it, the more I decided that she was right, at least sort of. I like T.J. We have a lot in common. He's fun to be around, and he challenges me. I don't know if we'll be together forever, but right now it's good. Even if we do end up going different ways at some point, we've had a great time together, and I think we've both learned a lot about who we are and what we want."

Jane stared at Cooper for a moment, blinking. "When did you become so mentally well?" she asked.

"I know it sounds really New Agey," said Cooper. "But it's the only way I can look at it without it all seeming like a giant disaster in the making. I'm trying to be realistic about it. No, I honestly don't believe that the guy I'm with when I'm sixteen is going to be the guy I'm with when I'm twenty-six, or thirty-six, or seventy-six. I'm not even convinced that the guy I'm with when I'm thirty-six will be the guy I'm with when I'm seventy-six. Look at my parents."

"But you're still doing it," Jane said.

Cooper nodded. "Right," she said. "I'm still doing it." She paused, thinking for a minute before continuing. "I used to spend a lot of time alone," she said. "Before I met Annie and Kate I sort of prided myself on not needing anyone around me. But they showed me that I do. I need friends. I need people like them—and like you. Will all of us be friends forever? I hope so, but even if we aren't, we make each other's lives better right now. That's how I look at my relationship with T.J. If it ends at some point, I'll be sad. But I won't ever forget the things he and I have done together. If I hadn't taken a chance on him, I wouldn't have those things."

Jane pushed her hair back, and Cooper saw that her dark eyes were wet, as if she was about to cry. "I wish I could see it that way," she said. "But it hurts so much right now that all I can think about is how stupid I was to think that someone might fall in love with me."

"Hey," Cooper said. "Did you just say what I think you did? You don't think someone would fall in love with you? What kind of garbage is that?"

Jane sniffed, half laughing and half crying. "You *have* to say that," she said.

"Want to bet?" Cooper said. "You should hear some of the things I say to Annie and Kate. I'm serious. You're one of the coolest people I know. You're smart, and funny, and you play a mean guitar. Oh, and of course you're ravishingly beautiful. Let's not forget that."

Jane smiled, looking a little like the old Jane, Cooper thought. Jane wiped a tear from her cheek and sniffed. "You're a great liar," she said. "Thanks."

"Are you always this hard on yourself?" asked Cooper. "You're even worse than I am. Don't you know that in any breakup it's always the *other* person's fault?"

"I'm not so sure this time," said Jane. "I think I just tried too hard. I really wanted this to work out."

"This guy must have been something else to get your attention," remarked Cooper. "Where did the two of you meet? School?"

"No," Jane said. "We met at this community center I go to sometimes."

Cooper knew that Jane did some volunteer work at a community center after school. But as it was with most things in Jane's life, Cooper didn't know any of the details. She wanted to ask some questions now that Jane had brought it up, but she didn't think the time was right. "Was he cute?" she asked instead.

Jane nodded. "Blue eyes. Punky blond hair. Loved Green Day and bad 1980s metal bands." She laughed. "On our first date we went to one of those used-CD stores down on Ferguson and looked for Motley Crue records."

"Sounds dreamy," Cooper said emphatically, rolling her eyes and clutching her hands to her chest in imitation of a love-struck girl.

"It *was*," Jane said. "It was fun to do that with someone."

"You've done that with me," Cooper said.

"I know," said Jane. "But I didn't want to kiss *you*. I wanted to kiss Max."

"*Max!*" repeated Cooper. "Romeo's name was Max?"

Jane nodded. "As in Max from *Where the Wild Things Are*. It was, as they say, an assumed name."

"What was the real one?" asked Cooper. "It must have been something awful if Max was better. I'm guessing Percival, or maybe Lawrence."

"I never found out," said Jane quickly. "I just always used Max. And I thought it was adorable."

"Wow," Cooper said. "You really *were* into this guy."

"Yeah," Jane said, sighing. "I was. And for a while there it seemed to be mutual."

"Until last night," said Cooper.

"Until last night," Jane said. "We were at a party at the center. I thought we were having fun. Then, a couple of minutes before midnight, the ball fell a little early. Max said things just weren't working out. I ran out. It was all very Cinderella."

Jane began to cry, softly. Cooper got up and went to sit beside her on the bed. She put her arm around Jane's shoulder and gave her a hug. "Hey," she said. "You've still got me."

Jane leaned her head against Cooper's shoulder. "That and thirteen bags of Oreos should just about get me over this," she said.

Cooper raised an eyebrow. "I'll go get the milk," she said, making Jane laugh.

They sat together for a few minutes, neither of them speaking. Cooper could feel Jane breathing, and Jane's head rested on her shoulder. She and T.J. had sat like that many times, usually when one of them was trying to make the other one feel better. She hoped it was making Jane feel a little bit better.

After a minute Jane reached out and took Cooper's hand. She squeezed it gently. "Thanks," she said. "I needed this."

Cooper squeezed Jane's hand back. "That's what friends are for," she said. "Who else would keep it a secret that you ate thirteen bags of Oreos?"

Jane sat up and sighed.

"Feel better?" Cooper asked her.

"A little," Jane said. "It will take a while. I'm not exactly the kind to let pain go right away, you know? I like to keep it around. Sort of like those people who save their gum to chew on later."

"Been there," Cooper said. "Take as long as you want. But in the meantime, don't call Max, okay?"

"How'd you know I was thinking about that?" Jane asked, sounding truly surprised.

"Please," Cooper said. "And pass up a moment of self-torture? Look who you're talking to."

Jane held up her hands in a gesture of surrender. "I bow to the master," she said. "And I promise, no calling."

"Or E-mail," Cooper said.

"Geesh, you're tough," said Jane. "Fine. No E-mail. No nothing. I swear."

"That's my girl," said Cooper, stroking Jane's hair. "Now, can we play some music? I've been working on some new stuff, and I want to hear what you think of it."

"Sure," Jane said. "I think I'm past the point of breaking into tears over sappy lyrics."

Cooper swatted her friend. "And just who writes sappy lyrics?" she demanded to know.

Cooper got up and retrieved her guitar. Sitting down in the chair, she began playing a song she'd been working on for a few days. Jane listened carefully, nodding her head and occasionally frowning slightly. When Cooper was done, she looked at Jane. "Well?"

"I like it," Jane said. "The chord progression is really cool. But I think the second verse needs some work, and maybe the chorus has some tiny little problems."

"Oh, is that all?" Cooper said.

"Relax," said Jane. "It's great. It just needs polishing." She picked up her own guitar. "I'm thinking something like this." She began playing, altering Cooper's melody just slightly. Cooper listened, then began playing along with her.

They were working on the chorus when there was a knock on the door. The girls stopped playing and Jane went to see who was there. When she opened it, Mr. Goldstein was standing there.

"There's someone here to see you," he said. "One of your friends."

"One of my friends?" Jane said. She looked back at Cooper with an expression of surprise.

Mr. Goldstein stepped aside and someone else stepped into the doorway. It was a girl. She was a little shorter than Jane, and she had short blond hair that stuck up as if it had been messed up with the utmost care. She was wearing faded jeans and a white T-shirt beneath a green bomber jacket.

Mr. Goldstein shuffled off down the hall, leaving the girls alone. Jane glanced back at Cooper, then looked at the girl. "What are you doing here?" she asked.

The girl shrugged. "I just thought I'd come by and see how you are," she said. "I didn't know you had company." She looked past Jane and nodded at Cooper. "Hey," she said.

"Hey," said Cooper. "Cool boots," she added, indicating the Doc Martens the girl had on. They were covered with stickers for various rock bands, and the toe of one of them was held together with silver electrical tape.

"Thanks," the girl said. "By the way, I'm Max."

"I'm Coop—" Cooper began to say, then stopped. Had she heard the girl correctly? Had she said that her name was Max?

"Coop?" the girl said, as if she hadn't heard correctly.

"Cooper," Jane said quickly. "It's Cooper."

"Cool," Max said. Then she looked back at Jane. "So, can we talk?"

Jane turned to Cooper, who was sitting there looking from Max to Jane and back again. Was this the same Max Jane had been talking about? As in the person she'd broken up with? But that meant that Max was—*a girl,* she told herself. Which meant that Jane was—

"We're kind of in the middle of something," Jane said.

Cooper shook her head, trying to regain her composure. A dozen different thoughts were running around in her head, and she was having a hard time remembering where she was. "That's okay," she said. "I mean, if you guys want to talk. . . ." She looked at Jane's face, searching for some clue to what Jane wanted. Jane nodded slightly.

"I'll just go," said Cooper. She put her guitar in its case and her music notebook into her backpack. She picked both of them up and headed for the door. "It was nice to meet you," she said to Max.

"Same here," Max said.

"I'll walk you out," Jane said.

Cooper walked down the hallway, stopping to say good-night to Mr. Goldstein. At the door, she paused. Jane looked at her. "I didn't know how to tell you," she said.

Cooper shook her head. "Don't worry about it," she said.

"I wanted to," said Jane. "But—"

"It's okay," Cooper said, smiling. "Really. We'll talk about it later. Go talk to Max. But don't let her off the hook too easily or I'll be really pissed."

Jane smiled, looking more vulnerable than Cooper had ever seen her. Cooper reached out and hugged her. "Call me later," she said.

"You're sure?" Jane said softly as Cooper slipped through the door. "I mean really sure?"

Cooper turned back to face Jane. "I'm sure," she said. "*Really* sure."

CHAPTER 3

"When are you going back to school again?" Kate glared at her brother as he put an empty plate on the kitchen counter. She'd been looking forward to having a piece of cheesecake all afternoon, but Kyle had eaten it all, leaving nothing but crumbs and a dirty knife behind.

"Can I help it if I'm a growing boy?" Kyle said, grinning as he wiped the last bits of cheesecake from his mouth.

Kyle had been home from college since two days before Christmas. Normally, Kate would have enjoyed having him there, but they'd had a falling out at Thanksgiving after Kate had told Kyle about her involvement in Wicca and he'd made disparaging comments about it. As a result, things between them had been decidedly chilly. For Christmas, Kate had given him socks, and he'd given her a cheap bottle of stinky perfume.

"What's going on in here?" asked Mrs. Morgan, walking in to find her children looking like wild dogs circling one another.

"Kyle hogged all the cheesecake," Kate said.

"I offered her some!" Kyle protested. "She said she was trying to cut back." He grinned at Kate over their mother's head.

Kate glared at him. She'd had it. "Mom," she said. "Kyle got a tattoo." She'd promised Kyle she wouldn't say anything about the tattoo on his shoulder. He'd gotten it at the beginning of the school year, and had shown it to Kate only after making her swear not to breathe a word about it to their parents. But she was angry, and she knew telling her mother about the tattoo would be the one thing she could do to really get Kyle in trouble.

"Kyle!" Mrs. Morgan exclaimed, whirling around to confront her son.

"She's making it up," Kyle said. "Honest."

"It's on his left shoulder," Kate said, smiling sweetly at her brother and then turning and walking out of the kitchen as Mrs. Morgan started to yank Kyle's shirt up.

Kate walked upstairs, savoring the protests that issued from the kitchen as Kyle tried to talk his way out of the very deep trouble she knew he was in. *I'm sure he'll find some way to get even*, she thought as she went to her room, but she didn't care. She'd been trying to think of some way to make Kyle pay ever since he'd told her he thought witchcraft was a lot of nonsense.

She shut the door and popped a Macy Gray CD

into the player. Macy's gravelly voice filled the room as Kate flung herself onto her bed and stared at the ceiling. She was bored. Even worse, she was angry. She was angry at Kyle. And as much as she didn't want to admit it, she was angry at Annie. She'd been avoiding thinking about her friend and her boyfriend being together behind her back for a long time. But she couldn't ignore it any longer. She had managed to convince herself that everything was fine, but what her friend had done really hurt her, and knowing Annie had been about to kiss Tyler the night before had brought it all rushing back. Oddly, it hurt her more to think about Annie's part in it than to think about Tyler's. Boys did that kind of thing. Friends weren't supposed to. Especially not friends like Annie.

Kate had tried to get rid of her anger. She'd done meditations and rituals designed to help her release the unhappy feelings inside of her. And they'd helped. But obviously they hadn't put the fire out completely, and that bothered her. She wanted things to be the way they had been before, if not with Tyler, at least with Annie. They'd been through so much together that she knew they would always be friends, no matter what happened. But she also knew that she couldn't really forgive Annie as long as she had the anger inside of her.

Kate sighed. It seemed she was always trying to get rid of one negative feeling or another, always battling to be happy. First she'd had to break away from her old friends and her old ways of thinking in order to study Wicca. Then she'd had to deal with her parents' negative reaction to finding out she was going to the study group, and to their insistence that she see a therapist. Now there was Kyle—and the situation with Annie and Tyler. It seemed that just when she was starting to enjoy herself, something came along to ruin things. She'd really believed that Tyler was the perfect guy and that once she had her parents' permission to be in the study group everything would be fine. But it wasn't fine. It was hard.

Nobody told you it would be easy, she reminded herself. She thought back to the night when she, Annie, and Cooper had dedicated themselves to studying Wicca for a year and a day. Sophia had told them that it wouldn't always be easy. *Boy, was she right*, Kate thought. If she'd known that it would be as hard as it had been, she wasn't sure she would have ever gone through with the dedication ceremony.

But you did, she thought. And as difficult as it was to believe, the year and a day was almost up. There were only a few months left. Then it would be time for the official initiation, at which—if they chose to go through with it—the class participants would become real witches. Kate couldn't even think about that at the moment. It was such a big decision, and she felt so unprepared to make it. Some days she felt absolutely sure that she wanted to do it; others the idea of saying that she was a witch totally freaked her out.

Then there was her birthday. In less than a week she was going to turn sixteen. Sweet sixteen. *I don't see what's so sweet about it*, she thought. She knew her friends wanted to have a party for her. So did her parents. But she didn't want *anyone* to have a party for her. She didn't want to celebrate. Since she was a little girl she'd been looking forward to turning sixteen, to getting her license and being able to drive by herself, to being almost grown up. Now she wished more than anything that she could be a little girl again, to be the age where the biggest thing she had to worry about was what flavor of ice cream to order or what to wear to school. *Those kinds of problems I could handle*, she thought.

A knock on the door interrupted her thoughts. "Come in," she called out.

Her mother opened the door and peered inside. "Am I interrupting?" she asked.

"Only if you count crashing a pity party as interrupting," answered Kate.

Mrs. Morgan stepped into the room and shut the door behind her. She stood for a moment, looking around at the books and the posters and the clothes hanging on the back of Kate's chair. Then she sat on the end of Kate's bed. "So," she said, "are you going to tell me what you and Kyle are fighting about?"

"We're not fighting," Kate said.

Her mother laughed. "Good one," she said. "He must have done something big for you to spill the beans about that tattoo. The last time you squealed on him like that was when you were twelve and he read your diary. If I recall, you informed your father that Kyle had a girlie magazine hidden under his mattress."

"What did you do to him?" asked Kate. She hoped it was something awful, although she couldn't really think of anything her mother could do to Kyle that would be all that tragic.

"Don't worry about him," Mrs. Morgan said. "He's feeling pretty bad about himself right now. But I'm more concerned about you. Are you okay?"

Kate shrugged. No, she wasn't okay. But how could she tell her mother what was going on with her? So much of it had to do with Wicca, and while her mother had come really far in her understanding of witchcraft, Kate didn't think she was quite ready to talk about it in detail. And as for the thing with Annie and Tyler, there was no way she could talk about that. It was too embarrassing.

But she had to say something. Her mother was looking at her expectantly. Besides, Kate was glad that she'd come up to see what was going on. She hadn't done that in a while, and Kate knew it meant her mother was feeling closer to her. She took a deep breath and thought carefully about how to phrase her answer.

"Have you ever had something happen between you and a friend that changed the friendship?" she asked. "Not destroyed it, but changed it, made it hard to go back to the way things were before, even though you *really* wanted things to be the same?"

Her mother nodded. "I had a friend in college named Betsy Panatowski," she said. "We were roommates our first year there, and we did everything together. I pretty much thought of her as a sister. She even came to our house for Thanksgiving because her family lived too far away and she couldn't afford to go back."

"She's the one in the picture you have on your desk, right?" Kate asked. "The one where the two of you are wearing swimsuits?"

Her mother nodded. "That's her," she said. "That was taken the summer between our freshman and sophomore years, when Betsy came to stay at our cabin on the lake for a few weeks."

"So what happened?" Kate asked, suddenly curious.

"A few weeks after we returned to school, we got into a fight. I don't even remember what it was about, really. I think maybe something about her borrowing some clothes of mine or something like that. Anyway, we were both yelling and saying all kinds of things because we were mad. Then Betsy told me that the only reason she was friends with me was because she felt sorry for me. She said that I was ugly, and that people laughed at me when I wasn't around."

Mrs. Morgan stopped talking. Kate looked at her, wondering what she was thinking. Kate was trying to imagine someone telling her mother that she was ugly. It made Kate angry to just think about it. She was surprised when her mother smiled and laughed.

"Thinking about it now, it seems so stupid," she said. "But at the time it really hurt my feelings. I remember running out of the room and hiding in one of the shower stalls to cry. I didn't talk to Betsy for three days. We tiptoed around each other, trying to avoid one another. Finally she apologized. She said that she'd only said those things to hurt me, and that of course they weren't true. Well, I *knew* they weren't true. That wasn't the problem. The problem was that now I knew that she was capable of hurting me. Our friendship just wasn't the same after that, even though we still sometimes write to one another. And you know what? I bet she doesn't even remember saying those things."

"You should remind her," Kate said bitterly.

Mrs. Morgan smiled. "Believe me, there have been times when I've been tempted," she said. "But it's not worth it. Sometimes the price you pay for remaining friends with someone is accepting that letting them get close to you means that they can hurt you more easily than other people can. It's easier when our enemies hurt us than when our friends do it, because we expect it from people who don't like us. But when it comes from someone we care about—wow, can that hurt."

Kate nodded. *It sure does*, she thought. It would have been easier if Tyler had kissed someone else—

anyone else. *Even Sherrie*, thought Kate. But he'd kissed her best friend. And Annie had kissed him back. And as much as she wanted to let go of that, she couldn't.

"Is this something you want to talk about?" her mother asked.

Kate shook her head. "Not yet," she said. "But thanks. The story helped."

"I'm glad I could be of service," said her mother. "But I actually asked about you and Kyle. I'm assuming one thing has nothing to do with the other?"

"No," Kate said. "He was just being a jerk. That's all."

Her mother looked at her for a minute. Kate knew that she was waiting for Kate to tell her more. And part of Kate wanted to do that. *After all*, she reminded herself, *you said your resolution was to be honest. Here it is one day into the new year and already you're backing off.* But she wasn't really backing off, she argued with herself. She *had* told her mother that something was wrong. She just hadn't given her all the details.

"Okay," said Mrs. Morgan. "Well, I actually came up to tell you something. There's a whole other cheesecake sitting in the refrigerator. And it has your name written all over it. Want to join me for a piece?"

Kate grinned. "Now you're talking," she said. "But we'd better hurry. Kyle's probably eaten half of it by now."

"Don't worry about him," her mother said. "I don't think he'll *ever* do that again."

Kate got up and started to walk out of the room with her mother. As they reached the door the phone rang. Kate picked it up.

"Hello?" she said.

"Hi, it's me," said Annie.

"Oh, hi," Kate replied. She was surprised to hear Annie's voice. They had only called each other a couple of times since things had gotten weird, and then only to confirm plans they'd all made.

"Are you doing anything tonight?" Annie asked.

"I'm not sure," answered Kate. "Why?" They had Monday off from school because of the holiday, and she hadn't made any plans.

"I was wondering if you'd like to come over for girls' night," Annie said. "Cooper's coming, and we haven't had one in a long time."

Kate hesitated. She did want to go, but the coal inside of her was beginning to flare up again. She knew it would be easy for her to make up an excuse about having to do something with her family. But *that* would definitely qualify as being dishonest. Besides, maybe it was time she faced her feelings. She looked at her mother, who was watching her from the doorway.

"Sure," she said. "I'll be there. What time?"

CHAPTER 4

"I knew it!" Sasha said triumphantly. "I told you they were getting married." She took a bite of pizza and wiped her mouth. "So, when's the big day?"

"April ninth," Annie answered, sitting down on the floor of her bedroom with the rest of them.

"That's like a week before our initiation ceremony," Cooper said.

"Try four days before," said Annie.

"They're going to plan a wedding in three months?" Kate said. Having helped her mother plan several since Mrs. Morgan had started her catering business, she knew how long it took to pull one together.

"They're not doing anything big," said Annie. "They're going to have it here at the house."

"I can't believe they're getting married," Kate said. "It seems so fast."

"Grayson asked her yesterday morning," said Annie. "They were so excited that they drove back here to tell me and Meg."

"How is Meg taking it?" asked Sasha.

Annie shrugged. "She's thrilled," she answered. "*I'm* thrilled. It's just kind of a shock is all."

"Have you talked to Becka about it?" asked Cooper.

"Last night," said Annie. "They called her to tell her. She was half asleep, so I don't think it sunk in right away. But I talked to her after they did, and by then she'd woken up a little."

"You two will be sisters!" said Sasha excitedly. "That is so cool."

"That part I'm really excited about," Annie said. "Nervous, but excited."

"Wait a minute," Cooper said. "Someone is going to have to move. Who is it going to be?"

"No one has talked about that yet," Annie said carefully. "And I didn't want to spoil the mood by asking."

"But you *could* be moving to San Francisco?" Kate asked.

"I guess so," said Annie. "I'm trying not to think about that, though. I'm trying to be happy for Aunt Sarah."

"Well, I'm happy for everyone," said Sasha. "This is really cool. It's like a fairy tale or something, where the plucky spinster heroine gets her prince and everyone lives happily ever after."

"I don't think Aunt Sarah would like being called a spinster," said Annie, laughing.

"All I meant is that she's not a silly young thing," said Sasha.

"And it really is like a fairy tale, if you think about it," Cooper said. "Who would have thought that you'd go back to your old house, find this guy living there, and that he'd fall in love with your aunt? It definitely makes you believe in fate."

"And it doesn't hurt that he's one of your favorite writers," added Kate. "Just think, you'll get to read all his new books before anyone else does."

Annie nodded. "I know," she said. "It all seems like a dream come true, doesn't it?" She paused for a moment. "Do you guys really think that everything happens for a reason? I mean, is there really some big plan that we only get to see in little bits and pieces, or do we just tell ourselves that because it makes things easier?"

"I think things happen for reasons," Cooper said. "Look how we all became friends, for example. Kate did a spell that backfired, then she found our names in that library book."

"But that could have been coincidence," Kate argued.

"I know it *could* have been," Cooper replied. "I'm just saying that I don't think it was. I think there was a reason we all needed to meet each other. The book is just what made it happen."

"And look how I met you guys," Sasha added. "I came to Beecher Falls totally by accident. I could have gone anywhere. But I didn't, and then I met you guys and my whole life changed."

"Those are all good things, though," Annie said carefully. "What about the bad things that happen to us?"

"Like what?" Cooper asked her.

"Well, what about what happened to Sasha?" she said. "Wouldn't it have been better if she'd never had to run away from home in the first place?"

Sasha nodded. "I've thought about that, too," she said. "What happened to me was really hard, and I wouldn't wish it on anyone. But if it hadn't happened I would never have come here. I would never have met you guys. I would never have ended up living with Thea. Those are all really great things. I'm not saying that having a happy childhood and a happy family wouldn't have been great, too. But I really believe that this is the life I was meant to have, and that those bad things were all a part of it. They taught me a lot about myself and about people in general. Maybe someday I'll be able to help someone going through what I went through. I don't know. That's the part I can't see yet, I guess. But I don't wish things had been any different, because I like who I am and I know that I am who I am because of what I went through." She stopped and laughed gently. "Wow. I sound like Oprah or something."

"You're thinking about your parents, aren't

you?" Cooper asked Annie, who had remained silent after Sasha's little speech.

"Yes," said Annie. "I was thinking about Midsummer, when the Oak King told me that there was some reason for my parents' deaths. I was furious at him for saying that. But maybe he was right. If they hadn't died, I would never have come here. Grayson and Becka would never have moved into our house. We would never have gone back to San Francisco and met them. And Aunt Sarah wouldn't be getting married. But it's really hard for me to believe that they had to die so that these things could happen."

"I don't think you can look at it that way," Cooper told her. "They didn't have to die so that these things could happen. And these things didn't happen because they died. They're just all connected. One thing leads into another, but it's not like we're all just acting out some big play that somebody else wrote."

"How do you know that for sure?" asked Annie. "We can think anything we want to, but how do we know? How do we know our lives aren't already planned out for us?"

"By who?" Kate asked her.

Annie shrugged. "I don't know. The Fates. The Goddess. Whoever."

"I don't buy that," Cooper said. "I think we're given a path to walk, but I think that path has lots of different side paths. We choose the ones we want to go down. I think people who say that everything happens whether you like it or not are just looking for something to blame for the fact that they don't like how their lives have turned out. There's a big difference between something happening for a reason and something being an excuse."

"Maybe," Annie said.

"How did this get so deep?" Sasha commented. "Usually we just talk about boys and clothes."

Cooper picked up a pillow and hit her with it. "You mean usually *you* just talk about boys and clothes."

"Sasha's right," said Annie. "I didn't mean for things to get all serious. I think it's time to up the fun quotient. And I think I know just the thing. Ice cream, anyone?"

"Count me in," Sasha said instantly.

The others nodded. "I'll go get it," Annie said. "But someone has to help me carry it up. Any volunteers?"

"I will," said Kate, standing up.

"Okay then," Annie said. "We'll be right back."

The two of them left the room and went down the stairs to the kitchen. Annie headed to the refrigerator and opened the freezer, removing two cartons of ice cream.

"What do you think?" she asked Kate, holding them up. "Vanilla or double fudge?"

"How about both?" suggested Kate, and Annie grinned.

"Get the bowls," she said.

Kate opened the cupboard while Annie removed the tops on the ice cream cartons. As Kate set four bowls on the counter she paused. "Annie," she said. "I—" She hesitated, and Annie looked at her, not saying anything.

Kate sighed. "I know it's been really hard lately. You know, between us."

"Kate, it's okay," Annie said.

"No," Kate said. "It isn't. It's not okay at all." She looked up into Annie's face. "I've been trying to pretend that everything is fine, that I'm not angry about what happened between you and Tyler. But I *am* angry. I'm really angry."

She stopped, unsure of how to continue. Annie said nothing as she waited to hear what her friend had to say.

"I know you never meant to hurt me," Kate said after a moment. "But you did, and we can't take that back. Sometimes I think I've gotten over it, like when we went away together for the Winter Solstice, but then I think about it and get mad all over again."

"Kate, if I could change what happened, I would," Annie said. "You don't know how many times I've wished I could do that."

Kate sniffed, feeling tears forming in her eyes. She smiled. "I know you would," she said. "That's the funny thing. I know that you'd do anything for me. I guess that's why what you did is even harder to let go of. I wish I could hate you, Annie. I wish I could look at you and not care if I hurt you right back. But I do care. You're a great person, and a great friend."

Neither of them spoke as they stood looking at one another. Kate felt a tear slide down her face, and she reached up to wipe it away. "Maybe this is just one of those things that had to happen," she said quietly. "Maybe it pushed all of us in the directions we needed to be going in. I just wish it didn't feel so bad."

"Just tell me what to do, Kate," Annie said, starting to cry herself. "Tell me what will make you feel better."

"You could jump in front of a train," Kate suggested. "That might help."

Annie stared at her in disbelief. Then Kate smiled. "Okay, maybe not. I just wanted to see your expression."

"But you've *thought* about me jumping in front of a train," Annie said. "I can tell."

Kate shrugged. "Not a train," she said. "But maybe I *did* think about you being eaten by bears. Just for a minute, though. And you went really quickly."

Annie looked shocked. Then she cleared her throat and said, "Well, as long as it made you feel better."

They both laughed. Then Kate held out her arms and Annie hugged her.

"I'm still mad," Kate said. "But I'm glad we're friends."

"So am I," said Annie. "But let's not do this again, okay?"

"As long as you keep your lips off my boyfriends, I don't see why we have to," replied Kate.

They separated and Annie looked at her friend. "You're right," she said. "You *are* still mad."

"I'm working on it," answered Kate. "Now, let's get this ice cream up there before those two come looking for us."

They dished the ice cream into the bowls and put them on a tray. Annie added a bottle of chocolate sauce and they returned to her bedroom.

"Finally," Sasha said as the two of them came in. "We were beginning to think you guys were eating it all yourselves."

"We were just having a moment," Kate said as she handed a bowl to Cooper.

Cooper took a bite of ice cream. "Speaking of moments," she said, "I had one myself this afternoon."

"Oh, do tell," said Kate.

Cooper poured chocolate sauce over her ice cream. "I wasn't going to say anything," she said. "But since we all seem to be in a sharing mood, I think I will. You guys have to swear it won't leave this room, though."

The other three looked at each other. "This must be big," Sasha said. "She never makes us swear."

"I'm serious," said Cooper. "I'm not saying a word unless you guys swear."

"We swear," Annie said. "Right, guys?"

Kate and Sasha nodded, looking at Cooper expectantly. Cooper set her bowl down.

"Okay," she said. "It's about Jane."

The others waited, spoons poised in midair. Cooper wiped her mouth with her hand. "I think she's a lesbian."

"Jane's a lesbian?" Sasha said. "Get out."

Cooper nodded. "I said I *think* she is. We haven't actually talked about it."

"What happened?" Kate asked. "I mean, how do you know?"

"I went over there this afternoon, and she was really down. She didn't want to tell me what happened, but I dragged it out of her. It turns out she got dumped by this person she was seeing—Max. Well, Max showed up and turned out to be a girl."

"He did *not*," said Annie. "I mean, she did not."

"She did," Cooper replied.

"Are you sure?" asked Kate, and Cooper gave her a withering look. "Well, you can't always be sure these days," Kate protested. "Maybe it was a guy who looked sort of girlie."

"Now I remember why I thought you were ditzy when I first met you," said Cooper. "No, this was a girl. Definitely a girl."

"A girl named Max," Annie said. "I can see why you didn't get it at first."

"Was she pretty?" asked Sasha.

"What?" Cooper said.

"Max," Sasha repeated. "Was she pretty?"

Cooper thought for a minute. "Yeah," she said. "She was kind of hot. Not pretty, but really cool looking. To tell the truth, I was so surprised I didn't really think about it all that much. She had really cool boots."

"I can't believe it," said Kate. "Jane's a lesbian."

"She might be bi," Annie suggested, and the others looked at her in surprise.

"What?" she said. "Like I don't know what being bi is? I listen to Ani DiFranco, thank you very much. And why shouldn't Jane be bi?"

"No," Cooper said. "You're right. Maybe she is. Like I said, we haven't actually talked about it. To tell the truth, I'm not really sure what to say."

"Why not?" asked Sasha. "You know other gay people. Isn't T.J.'s brother gay?"

Cooper nodded. "Dylan," she said. "But I don't know any girls who are gay."

"Yes, you do," Annie said.

The others looked at her again. "Something you want to tell us?" Sasha asked.

Annie blushed. "No," she said. "But there are a couple of lesbians in class. Oh, and there's that woman in the Coven of the Green Wood."

"How do you know all this?" asked Cooper. "Are you like the official lesbian registrar or something?"

"Ha ha," Annie retorted. "No, I just notice

people, I guess. It's not like it's any big deal."

"Well, I think it's a big deal to Jane," Cooper said. "And I want to talk to her about it. I just don't know quite how to do it."

"Just talk to her," Kate said. "She's your friend, right?"

Cooper nodded.

"Well, she's still your friend," said Kate. "Don't treat her any differently than you have been."

Cooper nodded and continued to eat her ice cream. After a minute Sasha said, "Are you afraid she might have a thing for you?"

Cooper choked on her double fudge. "No!" she said. "That hadn't even occurred to me."

Sasha shrugged. "It would occur to me," she said.

"Why should Jane have a crush on me just because she's a lesbian?" asked Cooper.

"Or bi," Annie said.

Sasha rolled her eyes. "I didn't say she *had* to have a crush on you," she said. "I just asked if you were worried about her having one."

"No," Cooper said. "At least, I don't think I am. Oh, Goddess, maybe I am. Does that make me a bad person?"

"Yes," Annie said.

"What is with you tonight?" Sasha asked Annie.

Annie took another bite of ice cream. "Just because Jane might be gay—"

"Or bi," Cooper said meaningfully.

"Or bi," Annie continued, "doesn't mean she

has a crush on every other girl in the world. That's ridiculous." She looked at Cooper. "Not that you're not *way* cute or anything."

"Thanks for the vote of confidence," Cooper said. "But none of this is really helping. What do I say to her?"

"Why do you have to say anything?" Kate said when no one spoke. "Just be her friend like you have been. That's what she really needs."

"You're right," Cooper said. "You're right. It just happened so fast is all. It took me by surprise."

"I think you're forgetting that this is about *Jane* and not about you," Annie said. "She'll probably be relieved that she can talk to you about it."

"I hope so," said Cooper. "We've gotten to be good friends. Not to mention that our music is really coming together."

"Hey," Sasha said thoughtfully. "Maybe now that Jane has this whole lesbian thing going on, the two of you can tour with Melissa Etheridge."

Cooper looked at her friend. Sasha grinned. "Annie's right," she said. "You are *way* cute. I bet the chicks will go for you in a big way."

"You are *so* dead when I finish this ice cream," Cooper said, trying to keep a straight face as the others hooted with laughter.

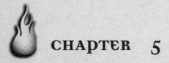 **CHAPTER 5**

As she stood waiting for Jane to answer the door the next afternoon, Cooper tried to remember everything she and her friends had talked about the night before. *Don't make a big deal out of this,* she reminded herself over and over. *And don't say anything stupid.*

The door opened and Jane looked out.

"Hey!" Cooper said brightly.

"Hey," Jane said. "Come on in."

Cooper went inside and followed Jane down the hallway to her bedroom. She opened her guitar case and took her guitar out. "I hope you're ready to play," she said. "I reworked that song and—"

"Cooper, we have to talk about yesterday," Jane said. She was sitting on the edge of her bed.

Cooper nodded. "Okay," she said. "What about it?"

"You can't tell me it didn't freak you out," Jane replied.

Cooper swallowed. "It was sort of a surprise, yeah," she said. "I mean, when you said Max I immediately assumed it was a guy."

"You don't know how hard it was not to use any pronouns," said Jane. "It's really a drag when you only have *he* and *she* to choose from."

Cooper laughed. "How did things work out, anyway?" she asked. "Are you two—" She paused, not knowing how to phrase her question.

"We're not going out, if that's what you mean," said Jane. "Max came by to tell me that she's not into dating anyone seriously right now." She rolled her eyes. "Like I am."

"Are you okay?" asked Cooper.

Jane shrugged. "I will be," she said. "But I'm not really worried about that right now. I want to know how you feel about all of this."

"Oh, I'm cool with it," Cooper answered quickly. "Really."

Jane narrowed her eyes. "Come on," she said, "You must have *some* questions. No one is that together. At least no one I want to hang out with."

Cooper grinned. "Okay," she said. "Maybe I do have a few questions."

"Shoot," said Jane. "I'll give you my best answers."

"Does this mean you only like girls?" asked Cooper.

Jane hesitated. "Let's just say I'm leaving my options open," she said. "I never really dated anyone before Max, so I can't say for sure that I'll never date guys. But if I had to give an answer to that one, I'd have to say that I'm strongly leaning toward being a big old lesbo."

Cooper looked at Jane with a surprised expression. "Can you say that?" she asked, making Jane laugh.

"Why not? It's not like I'm making fun of the Pope or anything. If there's one thing I've learned since I started going to the center, it's that you need to laugh at yourself every so often."

"The center," Cooper said. "As in the community center where you volunteer?"

Jane nodded. "The part I never told you was that it's a *lesbian and gay* community center. I've been going to a support group for young people there for a couple of months now. That's where I met Max. Okay, next question."

"This sounds stupid," Cooper said. "But how do you know? I mean, how do you know you're really gay?"

Jane sighed. "That's a tough one, and I'm not sure I can explain it all that well. The best way to answer it is to ask you how you know you're straight."

"I just do," Cooper said.

"Have you ever thought about being gay?" Jane asked.

Cooper shook her head. "Not really," she said. "I mean once I had a dream about making out with Gwen Stefani, but that's about it."

"That's sort of how it is with me," said Jane. "I can't really tell you how I know because it's more like I never *didn't* know. Ever since I was little I always imagined myself with girls, the way you probably imagined yourself with boys. It wasn't until I was older that I realized most other people thought that was different."

"Does your family know?" asked Cooper.

Jane shook her head. "No," she said. "No one knows except you, and I'd like to keep it that way for now."

Cooper felt an uneasy feeling growing in her stomach. She knew it had taken a lot for Jane to have this conversation with her, and she didn't want to do anything to make her friend feel uncomfortable. But she also knew that she had to tell her the truth.

"I sort of mentioned it to the girls last night," she said.

Jane's face fell. "You what?" she asked.

"I didn't mean to do anything wrong," explained Cooper. "It's just that I wasn't sure what to say to you, and we were all talking about—"

Jane was staring at her in disbelief. "I can't believe you would do that," she said, her voice trembling. She stood up. "I think you should go," she said.

"Jane," Cooper said. "I didn't mean—"

"Please," Jane said. "I can't be around you right now."

Cooper looked at her friend helplessly. She wanted Jane to tell her that it was okay, that she hadn't made a mistake. But she knew deep down that she had. She should never have told Kate, Sasha, and Annie about what had happened.

Without saying anything else, Cooper put her guitar back in its case and picked up her backpack. She looked at Jane, but Jane looked down at the floor. More than anything Cooper wanted to tell her how sorry she was, but she had a feeling that would only make things worse. Instead, she walked out of the room and down the hall. Jane didn't follow her as she went to the front door and left.

Cooper got into her car and started the engine. She gave the Goldsteins' front door one last look as she pulled away. *You've really done it this time*, she berated herself as she drove down the street. How was she going to make it up to Jane? What could she say to make it better? Her mind raced as a dozen different ideas came and went, none of them helpful. She just wanted to fix her mistake. But maybe she couldn't. Maybe she'd done the unforgivable. *I wonder if this is how Annie felt when she had to tell Kate about kissing Tyler*, she thought sadly.

She drove to T.J.'s house, where she parked and walked to the door. Mrs. McAllister answered her knock, greeting Cooper with a big smile and a cry of "Happy New Year!"

"Happy New Year," Cooper replied, returning the hug Mrs. McAllister gave her. "How were your holidays?"

"Busy," Mrs. McAllister said. "All the boys were

here. I just got rid of them a few hours ago. All except T.J., of course. He's around here somewhere."

Too bad Dylan isn't still here, Cooper thought as she removed her coat and said hello to Mac, the old Irish setter who had taken up what seemed like permanent residency at one end of the sofa. *I bet he'd have some good advice for me about how to talk to Jane.*

A moment later T.J. came down the stairs. He greeted Cooper with a kiss. "What's up?" he asked. "I didn't think I'd see you until tomorrow at school."

"I was in the neighborhood," Cooper lied.

T.J. cocked an eyebrow. "Why don't I believe you?" he asked.

"All right," said Cooper. "I give. I came over to see if you wanted to go for a walk."

"With you?" asked T.J.

Cooper hit him in the arm. "No, with your other girlfriend," she said.

T.J. rubbed his arm. "I don't know," he said. "I'll have to ask her if she's busy."

"Keep it up, pal," said Cooper. "Next time I'll show you what I learned in self-defense class."

"Ow," T.J. said, backing away.

"Go get your coat," ordered Cooper.

T.J. went away and came back a minute later, dressed in his old leather jacket. Cooper retrieved her jacket from the couch and the two of them left the house.

"I'm assuming you want to talk about something,"

T.J. said as the two of them walked along the sidewalk. "Or did you just miss me?"

"You wish," replied Cooper affectionately. "No, I wanted to ask you something."

"Something good or something bad?"

"Neither, really," answered Cooper. "I need some advice."

T.J. stopped and looked at her. "*You* asking for advice?" he said incredulously. "From *me*?" He bent down and touched the ground.

"What are you doing?" asked Cooper.

"I wanted to see if hell had frozen over," said T.J.

Cooper kept walking, and T.J. trotted to keep up with her. "Okay," he said. "I'm all ears."

Cooper wasn't sure how to proceed. She wanted to talk to T.J. about the situation with Jane. But she'd already caused enough trouble by telling Annie, Kate, and Sasha about it. Would she just be making it worse if she told T.J., too? *It's not like he's going to tell anyone*, she argued with herself. That part was true. If there was anyone who could keep something quiet, it was T.J. But telling him would still be letting one more person in on Jane's secret. She decided to try the middle road.

"Do you remember when Dylan told you he was gay?" she asked.

T.J. gave a short laugh. "Actually, he didn't," he answered. "Some kids in the neighborhood told me. I believe their exact words were, 'Hey, did you know your brother is a big fag?'"

"What?" said Cooper, shocked.

T.J. nodded. "I got into a big fight over that one. Then I went home and told my mom what they'd said. I still remember the look on her face when she told me to sit down at the kitchen table. She wiped the blood off my nose with a damp dish towel. Then she told me about Dylan. I ran out of the kitchen and hid up in my room. I beat my pillow over and over, pretending it was the face of the kid who had said that about my brother. But really I think I was pretending it was Dylan."

"Why?" asked Cooper.

T.J. sighed. "I was really angry at him," he answered. "I didn't want him to be different. I didn't want him to be a fag, like that kid called him. I wanted him to be normal."

"But gay people *are* normal," Cooper said.

"I know that now," said T.J. "But then all I knew was that my brother—the guy I looked up to—was something that some people thought was wrong. It took me a while to realize that I was the one who was wrong. It took all of us a while, my dad in particular."

"But he's okay with it now, right?" asked Cooper.

"More or less," said T.J. "He doesn't really talk about it very much. He and Dylan talk about work and cars and that kind of stuff. I think that's the best he can do." T.J. paused. "Do you mind if I ask why the sudden interest in this?"

"I kind of found out by accident that someone I know is gay," said Cooper, trying to be as general as possible.

"I see," said T.J. "And you're having trouble with it?"

"Oh, no," said Cooper. "I'm fine with it. But I kind of mentioned it to some other people, and now the first person is really mad at me."

T.J. gave a low whistle. "Now I get it," he said. "You broke rule number one—never tell anyone without permission."

"I didn't mean to," said Cooper defensively. "It just sort of came out. Pardon the pun," she added after realizing what she'd just said.

"Outing someone is about the worst thing you can do," T.J. told her. "Especially if the person is just figuring it out herself or himself. That's what happened to Dylan. He told one of his best friends, and he told a bunch of other people who shouldn't have known."

"Okay," said Cooper. "I get it. I screwed up. The question is, what do I do now? How do I fix this?"

"I don't know," T.J. answered.

"What do you mean you don't know?" exclaimed Cooper. "I thought the whole idea of this little chat was for you to help me out."

"Sorry," T.J. said. "But I don't know this person. I don't know how he or she is feeling, or what his or her situation is."

"Stop with the he/she thing already," said

Cooper impatiently. "Jane was right, it's a real pain."

"Jane?" T.J. said as Cooper realized, too late, what she'd said. "Are we talking about Jane?"

Cooper groaned. "See?" she said. "That's how it happens. There I was, being all careful not to say anything."

T.J. grabbed her and put his arms around her. "Don't worry," he said. "I'm not going to breathe a word of this."

Cooper laid her forehead against his chest. "Good," she said. "It's bad enough that I told the girls. If Jane knew that I told you, too, she'd totally freak. As it is she'll probably never speak to me again anyway."

T.J. hugged her tightly. "Give her some time," he said. "I bet she'll come around. The important thing is that she knows *you* aren't freaked out by this. You're not, are you?"

"Maybe a little," Cooper said softly. "And that makes me feel even worse."

"You're allowed to be freaked out," T.J. said. "Everybody wants to seem all cool and okay with it, but this is all new information to you. You need some time to get used to it. So give each other some space. Call her in a couple of days and see where things stand. My bet is that she'll be glad to hear from you."

Cooper nodded. "It's a plan, then," she said. "Thanks."

"Good," said T.J. "Now there's something I

want to talk to *you* about."

"You mean this isn't all about me?" Cooper said, frowning.

"Sadly, no," T.J. answered. "But it is about us."

"That sounds bad," sad Cooper.

"I don't have to tell you if you don't want to hear it," T.J. suggested.

"No," said Cooper. "Tell. Otherwise I'll just make up something worse."

They began walking again, with Cooper holding T.J.'s hand.

"My parents are starting to talk about college," T.J. said.

Cooper groaned. Her own parents had begun making noises about the same subject. She'd managed to put them off, largely because they were still dealing with their divorce, but she knew the day was coming when she'd have to address the issue.

"And?" Cooper said.

"And they really want me to think about going to school in Minnesota," said T.J. "To Rummond."

Cooper didn't respond. She'd known for a long time that the McAllisters really wanted T.J. to go to Rummond University. It's where Mr. McAllister had gone. They'd hoped that one of the other boys would go, but each had chosen another school. T.J. was their last hope for sending another McAllister to the old alma mater.

"And what do you want?" Cooper asked.

"I'm not sure," answered her boyfriend.

"Rummond has a great English department. I've been thinking about majoring in creative writing."

"What about music?" Cooper inquired.

"Music is fun," said T.J. "But really, what are the chances of making a career out of it?"

"I don't know," Cooper said. "Why don't you ask Dave Matthews . . . or Bono?"

"Come on," T.J. said, squeezing her hand. "You know what I mean. I have to be at least a little bit practical."

Cooper sighed. "I guess I thought we'd have longer before we had to think about all of this," she said.

"They keep leaving school brochures on my desk," said T.J., chuckling. "And for Christmas my dad gave me a Rummond sweatshirt. Very subtle, huh?"

Cooper had to laugh, even though inside she was starting to feel a little sad. They weren't even done with their junior year, and already people were pressuring them to make decisions about what they were doing after graduation. *Next they'll be asking me what I want to be when I grow up*, she thought bitterly.

"So?" T.J. said. "Any thoughts?"

"About Rummond?" Cooper said. "You're right, it's a good school."

"I don't want your opinion about Rummond," T.J. replied. "I want to know what you think about us maybe going to separate schools."

Cooper didn't answer. She *couldn't* answer. The

truth was, she hadn't really allowed herself to think about it in much detail. She'd always known that the time would come when they'd have to make this decision, and she'd always assumed that when it came she'd know just what to do. But now that it was here, she found that she didn't.

She gripped T.J.'s hand a little more tightly. "Can I get back to you on this?" she asked. "I think I can only handle one crisis at a time."

CHAPTER 6

"Astrology has been around for thousands of years."

Olivia Sorensen stood in front of the class at Crones' Circle. She was clearly nervous, and she kept playing with her glasses as she spoke and took frequent sips from the glass of water that Sophia had put on the table for her.

"No one is exactly sure how people first became interested in the stars and planets and their effects on our lives," she continued. "But we know that every ancient civilization had some system of astrology. The Mayans. The Egyptians. The Greeks. All of them followed the movements of the celestial bodies. And what is really intriguing is that even though these cultures were separated by thousands of miles, and sometimes many years, they all basically had the same ideas about how the stars and planets worked."

Olivia pointed to a poster that hung on the wall, showing the different phases of the moon. "Take this moon calendar, for example," she said. "Many of you probably have similar ones at home."

Annie nodded. She herself had a beautiful moon calendar that her friends had given her for her birthday. She loved tracking the moon as it went from dark to full to dark again. Sometimes she timed her rituals and meditations to the various phases.

"Why are we so interested in the full moon?" Olivia asked the class. "Why do we pay attention to when the moon is waxing and waning?"

"Because it reminds us of the Goddess?" suggested a woman in the back. "It symbolizes how she represents birth, death, and rebirth."

Olivia nodded. "That's one reason," she said. "But I'm talking about the moon's effect on different aspects of our lives."

"You mean like the tides," Annie said. "The way the high and low tides change with the phases of the moon and how close it is to the earth."

Olivia nodded. "Exactly," she said. "For centuries fishermen and sailors have charted the moon's course because they know it affects the tides and the currents. It also affects other things."

"Like what?" asked a man to Annie's left.

"Well, like women's menstrual cycles," Olivia said. "Many women find that their periods follow the moon's cycle. And what about animals? Haven't you ever heard dogs or wolves baying at the full moon?"

"Isn't that just an old wives' tale?" asked Kate. "You know, like werewolves coming out when the moon is full?"

"Yes and no," Olivia replied. "There's a lot of scientific evidence that the moon does affect how people behave. For example, many hospital emergency rooms report an increase in cases on nights when the moon is full, and it's been shown that people's brain waves do sometimes change with the moon's phases."

"What does all of this have to do with astrology?" someone asked.

Olivia held up her finger. "I'm getting to that," she said. "Many of you probably think of astrology the way most people think of it—as the horoscopes you read in the paper."

A lot of heads nodded in response to her statement, and several people laughed. Olivia smiled.

"Obviously, horoscopes are part of astrology," she said. "Unfortunately, they're probably the most unreliable part. At least the ones you read in the papers are. The problem is that those horoscopes have to be very general, so that they can be applied to as many readers as possible. Yes, there is some useful information in them, if you know how to use it correctly. But essentially newspaper horoscopes are about as in-depth as your typical supermarket tabloid is."

"That's too bad," Cooper remarked. "Mine said I was going to have good luck in all things today."

Olivia smiled. "When's your birthday?" she asked.

"April twenty-eighth," Cooper told her.

"Taurus," Olivia said. "The bull." She thought for a minute. "Actually, your luck right now probably isn't so great," she said. "My guess is that you're finding yourself running into a few obstacles that you feel like charging right through but know you can't."

Cooper nodded approvingly. "Actually, that's pretty much it," she said. "How'd you know?"

Olivia adjusted her glasses. "I sort of cheated," she said. "I could have said the same thing for everyone in this room, and for everyone on the planet, actually. Right now we're in what's called a Mercury Retrograde period."

"A what?" Annie asked, trying to write down what Olivia was telling them.

"Mercury Retrograde," Olivia said. "It's something that happens two or sometimes three times a year when the planet Mercury appears to move backward in its orbit for a short period of time, usually about three weeks."

"And what does that mean in the real world?" Cooper asked her.

"Mercury, as you probably know, was the messenger of the gods," Olivia explained. "The planet Mercury, which is named for him, has an enormous influence on things like communication and travel. So when Mercury starts to go backward, things relating to those two areas get a little mixed up."

"Mixed up how?" asked Kate.

"Well," Olivia said, "it could be a lot of different things. You might have more misunderstandings than usual with people. You might find that you have trouble meeting deadlines for projects, or that your computer breaks down for no apparent reason."

"That happened to me yesterday!" said one of the men in the class. "I got a new computer for Christmas, and for no reason it crashed while I was in the middle of writing a letter."

"That's classic Mercury Retrograde," said Olivia. "People report all kinds of problems with machinery during these periods. People who travel frequently find that their flights are delayed or the rooms they booked suddenly aren't available."

"Tell me about it," said Sophia, who was standing off to the side listening. "I had friends flying in for New Year's, and they were four hours late."

"Yeah, but that could have just been trying to fly on one of the busiest days of the year," Annie said. "And all of this other stuff—do you really think a planet's relative movement could cause all of this?"

"I see we have a skeptic," Olivia said.

"I'm not really a skeptic," Annie said, suddenly feeling self-conscious as everyone looked at her. "I just think it's too easy to blame things on forces we can't really measure."

"You're right," Olivia responded. "And some people do that. So let's try something. I want you to give me your birthday, along with the time of day you were born and the city. That's all I want to know. I'm going to work up a chart for you, and I'll bring it to class next time we meet. Then we'll see how accurate it is."

"Okay," said Annie. "That sounds like fun."

"It should be," Olivia said.

"What kinds of things will the chart tell us?" asked Kate.

"It will tell us general things about her personality," explained Olivia. "It should also be able to pinpoint some major events in her life. That's how astrologers know if they've plotted the chart correctly from the information they've been given."

"This should be very interesting," remarked Cooper, looking at Annie. "Now maybe we'll find out why she's so strange."

The class laughed. "Just call me with that information and I'll work up the chart," Olivia told Annie.

The rest of the class was spent discussing the various planets and what things they were believed to affect. Olivia handed out several pieces of paper with information on them, and then it was time to go. Annie, Cooper, and Kate helped put the room back in order, then said good-bye to Sophia and the others and headed out.

"That was something, huh?" Cooper said as they walked to the bus stop. "And lucky you," she added to Annie. "I can't wait to see what your chart says."

"I'm sure it will be a lot of generalities," responded Annie.

"You're not even the least little bit interested?"

Kate asked her. "I'm surprised."

"I'm interested," Annie said. "I just don't know if I believe that pieces of rock spinning around up in space can have any influence in my life."

"But you believe that you can do spells," Kate said. "How is that any different? You can't measure intention and energy, either."

"True," Annie admitted. "But I've experienced those things. And at least energy comes from within us. The idea that I'm at the mercy of Pluto and Mars isn't something I'm comfortable with."

"You're such a science nerd," Cooper teased. Then she put her arm around Annie's shoulders. "But that's why we love you. It's like we're our very own *Charlie's Angels*. You're the smart one who figures everything out. I'm the tough one."

"And I'm what?" Kate said warily. "If you say the pretty one, you'd better be ready to run fast."

"We're *all* the pretty ones," said Cooper tactfully. "I was going to say that you're the athletic one."

"That's better," Kate said happily.

"Although if we ever needed to go undercover at a fashion show, you *are* the one I'd send," Cooper added.

Kate chased her all the way to the bus stop, with Annie following them yelling, "Slow *down*." When they got there the bus was just pulling up. The three of them got on and collapsed into seats in the back, laughing so hard they couldn't breathe. When they finally regained their composure Annie said to

Cooper, "You never told us how things went with Jane yesterday."

"Badly," Cooper said, sobering up. "I really stepped in it. But I think things will be okay. I'm just giving her a few days to cool down."

"You should invite her to Kate's party this weekend," Annie suggested.

"Am I having a party?" asked Kate.

"It *was* going to be a surprise," Cooper said, smacking Annie's knee.

"Whoops," said Annie. "I forgot. Surprise!" she added, beaming at Kate.

"You shouldn't have," Kate said, feigning shock and delight. "So, what are we doing?"

"We're having a little get-together at my house," Annie said. "Saturday night. Is that okay?"

Kate nodded. "Mom has a catering thing that night, so we're doing the family thing on Sunday." *And my therapy appointment is in the morning, so that will be out of the way,* she thought to herself.

"It will just be us girls," Annie said. "Nothing too big."

"Sounds perfect," said Kate. "And by all means invite Jane," she added to Cooper.

"I will," Cooper replied. "And now here's our stop."

They got off and went in their respective directions. When Annie got home she found her aunt in the kitchen with Meg.

"Hey there," Sarah said. "I was just about to send someone off to bed."

"That would be me," Meg said. She gathered the homework she'd been working on and headed up to her room. Annie went to the refrigerator and poured herself a glass of water.

"Do you know where my birth certificate is?" she asked her aunt.

Sarah nodded. "It's in the fireproof box in the closet," she said. "Do you need it?"

Annie nodded. "It's nothing major," she said. "We're learning about astrology in class. The woman teaching us wants to do my chart, and I need to give her some information."

"How fun!" Aunt Sarah said. "Let's go get the birth certificate."

They went into Aunt Sarah's office and she opened the closet. It was piled with boxes, half of which tumbled out onto the floor.

"I'm going to have to do something about this mess before we combine households," she remarked as she shoveled some loose papers back into the boxes with her hands.

Annie almost took the opportunity to ask exactly *where* the households would be combining, but she didn't. Nor did her aunt say anything else about it. Instead she rooted around in the back of the closet, finally emerging with a metal box.

"Here it is," she said. She flipped the latch and

opened the box. Inside there were all kinds of papers. Aunt Sarah riffled through them. "Wills. Deed to the house. Marriage license," she said as she looked at the various papers. "Ah, here we are. Birth certificates." She took out a faded piece of paper and handed it to Annie. "There you go."

Annie looked at the paper in her hand. She'd never seen it before, and it felt weird to be holding the document of her birth. There was her name, and below it her parents' names and their signatures.

"You were born at two twenty-three in the morning," Aunt Sarah said. "I'll never forget it. Chloe went into labor at 8:00 in the morning the day before. We thought you'd be such an easy birth. But it was like you were determined to hang on until you were good and ready to come out. Your father was actually trying to coax you out by talking to your mother's belly."

Annie laughed. "I wish I remembered it," she said.

"You finally came out when he started singing to you," her aunt told her. "And we were all glad you did. Your father had a *terrible* voice."

"*That* I do remember," Annie said.

Aunt Sarah took the birth certificate and made a copy of it on the small copier next to her desk. She gave it to Annie and put the original back in the box, which she then returned to the closet.

"Thanks," Annie said. "I'll let you know what I find out about myself."

"I'm sure it's all good," Aunt Sarah said as they left her office and returned to the kitchen. Annie headed for the stairs, but her aunt called her back. "I want to talk to you about something," she said.

Annie sat at the kitchen table across from Aunt Sarah. Her aunt picked up a cookie from the plate on the table and nibbled at it. She offered one to Annie, but Annie shook her head. She was too worried about what her aunt was going to say to eat.

"I'm sure it's crossed your mind that someone will have to move when the wedding happens," her aunt said.

Annie nodded. "I kind of figured that different cities wouldn't be the way to go," she joked.

Aunt Sarah smiled. "I just want you to know that Grayson and I haven't made any decisions about that yet," she said. "There are a number of factors involved, and we're trying to weigh everything and decide what makes the most sense."

"Fair enough," Annie said.

Her aunt took another bite of cookie. "This is pretty weird, isn't it?" she said.

Annie nodded. "A little," she said. "Not in a bad way or anything. Just a little weird."

"It's funny how life works out," Aunt Sarah said thoughtfully. "I really never thought I'd get married. I always thought of the three of us as a little family. Now that family is going to get bigger. If someone had told me a year ago that this was going to happen I would have bet a million bucks they were wrong."

"Fate," Annie said softly.

"What?" her aunt asked.

"Oh, nothing," said Annie, realizing she'd spoken out loud. "It's just something Cooper said the other night."

Aunt Sarah nodded. "Anyway, I just wanted you to know that no one has made any decisions yet," she said. "And we won't without talking to you and Meg and Becka."

"Thanks," said Annie. "And whatever happens, I love you, Aunt Sarah."

"I love you, too," her aunt said.

Annie stood up, gave her aunt a kiss good-night, and went up the stairs to her room. She put the copy of her birth certificate on her desk. As she looked at it sitting there, at her parents' names below hers, she thought about everything that had happened to get her to where she was. *Is it really fate?* she asked herself. When she was honest, she had to admit that she didn't really know. Then she looked at the piece of paper on which Olivia Sorensen had written her number. *But maybe I'm about to find out,* she thought.

CHAPTER 7

"Still here?" Kate dropped her backpack on the floor next to the couch and walked past Kyle, who was sitting in one of the armchairs and holding the television remote in one hand as he flipped listlessly through the channels.

"Some of us don't have to go back until *next* week," he said. "That's one of the advantages of not being in high school anymore."

"I see," Kate called from the kitchen. "Along with not having to do any of your own dishes, apparently." She looked at the collection of plates, cups, and silverware in the sink and shook her head.

"I was going to get to those," said Kyle, coming into the kitchen.

"Right after you do all the laundry you left by the machine, clean the house, and do the grocery shopping to replace all the food you've been eating, right?" snapped Kate.

"All right," said Kyle. "What gives? You've been coming down on me ever since I got home. Not to mention snitching on me to Mom about the tattoo, which I'll probably never hear the end of."

Kate took a bite of the apple she'd pulled out of the refrigerator and gave Kyle a fake smile. "That just slipped out," she said. "Sorry."

Kyle groaned. "Just so you know," he said, "sarcasm is *not* attractive in a girl."

Kate stormed past him and out of the kitchen. Kyle followed her as she headed up the stairs. "I'm just kidding!" he called after her. "Talk to me, Kate."

Kate stopped on the stairs and wheeled around. Kyle was standing at the bottom of the steps, looking up at her.

"Okay," she said. "You really want to know what's bothering me?"

Kyle nodded. "Yeah, I do," he said.

"Fine," said Kate. "What's bothering me is that my brother has apparently turned into a narrow-minded, insensitive jackass."

Kyle's face fell, and he stared at her in confusion. "*What* are you talking about?" he asked. "What did I *do*?"

Kate crossed her arms over her chest. "What you did was make fun of me when I tried to talk to you about something important to me. But if you don't remember, I guess it's not that important to you."

Kyle shook his head as if he was trying to remember something. Then he looked up at Kate. "Are you talking about that witch stuff?" he asked.

Kate didn't reply. She continued to stare at him angrily.

"Come on, Kate," Kyle said. "Get over it already."

"See," Kate said, pointing a finger at him. "That's the problem. You think this is all some silly game. It's not important to you, so you think it can't possibly be important to me. Well, it is, Kyle. It's very important. It took a lot for me to tell you about the class, and about Mom and Dad sending me to therapy. And what did you do? You laughed at me."

She was so angry she was shaking. Kyle continued to stare at her as if he'd never seen her before. Kate wanted to turn and run away, to hide in her room so she wouldn't have to see him looking at her like that. *You wanted to tell the truth,* she reminded herself. *Nobody said that was going to be easy.*

"That's why you told Mom about my tattoo?" said Kyle. "Because I teased you about the witch stuff?"

Kate nodded. She could tell that her brother really didn't understand why she was so mad at him. That made her even more upset, but she knew letting her anger get out of control would make everything worse. She took a deep breath.

"I could always tell you anything," she said. "Even stuff I couldn't tell Mom and Dad. Then when I told you the one thing that I really wanted you to understand, you made me feel like an idiot."

Kyle looked away for a moment. When he turned back he shrugged his shoulders. "What can

I say?" he asked his sister.

"You can start by apologizing," Kate suggested.

"I'm sorry," Kyle said. "I guess I really thought this was just some crazy idea you had and you'd get over it."

"Well, it's not," said Kate. "It's really important to me, and if you'd bothered to listen to me you would have realized that."

Kyle put up his hands. "All right," he said. "So explain it to me."

Kate thought for a minute. Did she really want to try to explain Wicca to Kyle? She knew that no matter what he said, he still thought it was ridiculous. Would trying to change his mind just give him more ammunition to use against her the next time they fought? *Probably*, she told herself. *But you started this, and it's up to you to finish it.*

"Okay," she said. "Come on."

She turned and went to her room. She heard Kyle come up the stairs after her. He came into her room, where she was putting her stuff down and trying desperately to think of a way to talk to her brother about the Craft.

"Have a seat," she said, indicating her desk chair.

Kyle sat down and looked at her expectantly. Kate found herself growing more and more nervous. It was like she was giving a presentation in front of a thousand people who needed to be convinced that Wicca was a legitimate religion, not just talking to her brother. *I wonder if this is how Cooper felt when she had to speak to the school board*, she mused, thinking about the time her friend had to convince a lot of people that her wearing of a pentacle wasn't something they should be afraid of. How had Cooper done it? Where had she begun?

Start with your altar. A quiet voice echoed through her mind, like someone whispering to her from behind a curtain. The voice soothed her, and she felt her racing heart begin to slow down. A calmness began to replace the anxiety that had been roiling in her stomach. Suddenly she had an image in her mind of a woman standing behind her, smiling gently and encouraging her. She knew the woman was some kind of goddess, although she didn't know which one. But it didn't matter. The point was that it reminded her that she wasn't alone.

Start with the altar, Kate prodded herself. She turned to the small table she'd set up beside her bed. It wasn't anything fancy, because she hadn't wanted to freak her parents out too much while they were still getting used to the idea of her studying Wicca, but it did the job. She picked up the small statue that sat in the center of the altar and held it up.

"This is the goddess," she told Kyle, who stared at the statue blankly. "Well, one of them, anyway. This one happens to be Demeter."

"There's more than one?" Kyle asked, taking the statue from Kate and looking at it.

Kate nodded. "There are thousands of them,"

she said. "Although really they're all different forms of the same one. It's like there's one big Goddess and she has lots of personalities. At least that's how I like to think of it. Other people have their own ideas about it."

"What does this one do?" asked her brother, holding up the statue.

"Demeter is a nature goddess," Kate said. Her reservations about talking to Kyle about witchcraft were quickly disappearing as she tried to remember everything she could about Demeter. She had gotten the statue as a Yule gift from the women at Crones' Circle. Each class participant had been given a different goddess or god, and Kate had been particularly happy to receive Demeter. She'd always liked the story of the goddess, and as she told it to Kyle she found herself speaking easily.

"Demeter had a daughter named Persephone," Kate explained. "She loved her more than anything. The two of them used to walk through the fields together, and because Demeter was so happy the crops and flowers grew really well. Then one day, while they were walking, the fields opened up and the god Hades dragged Persephone down into the underworld."

"Why?" Kyle asked. He was studying the statue of Demeter closely.

"He was in love with her beauty," explained Kate. "He wanted her to be his wife."

"He couldn't just ask?" said Kyle.

Kate laughed. "The gods don't seem to do a lot of asking," she said. "He just sort of kidnapped her. Demeter was crushed. She walked all over the earth, asking people if they'd seen her daughter. In the meantime, Persephone was sitting around in the underworld being really freaked out about it all."

"Why didn't she just leave?" Kyle inquired.

"She couldn't," said Kate. "Hades wouldn't let her. Besides, there are all these guardians to the underworld, and they wouldn't let her get past. So she had to sit there while Hades tried to convince her that things weren't so bad. Also, I think Hades must have been kind of cute, and Persephone sort of liked him in that weird 'I shouldn't like you but I do' way. Anyway, back upstairs, Demeter was getting sadder and sadder, and the sadder she got the more the plants wilted. Finally nothing would grow and winter came for the first time. This didn't make the farmers all that happy, and they begged her to make everything grow again. Only she was so heartbroken that she couldn't."

"This all sounds like a giant soap opera," Kyle remarked.

"It gets better," said Kate. "Finally everyone was so miserable that they all asked Hades to let Persephone go. He agreed, but first he offered her a pomegranate."

"Why?" Kyle asked.

"Because no one had invented chocolate yet," Kate said smartly. "Well, Persephone ate a few of the seeds from the pomegranate. Then she went on her way out of the underworld and back to her mother. Demeter was so happy that immediately spring came and everything started to grow again."

"Let me guess," Kyle said when Kate paused. "There was a catch."

"Major catch," Kate told him. "Because Persephone had eaten the pomegranate seeds, she was forced to return to the underworld for part of the year. So she spent six months here and six months there. When she was down there moping around with Hades, Demeter got all sad again and winter came."

"And because no one had invented skis yet, this was a big bummer, right?" Kyle said.

"Right," Kate said. She took the statue of Demeter from him and placed it back on the altar. "So that's her story."

"And you have her on that table why?" Kyle asked.

"She reminds me that things change," Kate said. "Wicca is all about nature, and cycles, and how things are connected to one another. Having the statue there reminds me of that."

"And you do what with it?" Kyle said hesitantly.

"Sacrifice goats and things to it," said Kate, pretending to be serious.

Kyle stared at her in horror. Kate smiled sweetly. "Just kidding," she said. "But you almost bought it, right?"

Kyle turned red. "It's just that when you said you were into witchcraft—" he began.

"Relax," Kate said. "A lot of people have weird ideas about what witches do. So just to clear things up, no one sacrifices anything."

"Good to know," Kyle replied, sounding relieved. "So, what *are* you into?"

Kate sighed. This was the hard part. Explaining Wicca to people who hadn't ever experienced it themselves was difficult. Many people thought it was a lot more complicated than it was, and sometimes the truth was harder to accept than the fantasy.

"Well, I told you that there's the Goddess," Kate began. "She's like this big presence that's out there."

"Like God?" asked Kyle.

"Yes and no," Kate said. "I think it depends a lot on what you believe. There's no one way of thinking about her."

"How do *you* think of her?"

Kate bit her lip. "You're going to think this is really weird," she said.

"No weirder than I did before," Kyle retorted.

"Okay," Kate said. "Just bear with me. You know the big space station in *Star Wars*, the one that all the other fighter planes flew back and forth from?"

"Yeah," Kyle said, looking at her with a wondering expression.

"Well, I sort of think of the Goddess like that," Kate said.

"As the Death Star?" repeated Kyle. "Isn't that a

little creepy? I mean what with the whole inter-galactic evil thing and all?"

"Not as the Death Star itself," Kate said. "But as this big entity made up of lots of smaller entities. Each one of them has a different job, and she sends them out when she needs those jobs done. It's like the Goddess herself is too big for me to really think about without getting a little overwhelmed, like when you try to think of the ocean as *the ocean* or space as *space*, you know? But the little entities I can understand, like Demeter."

She paused, looking at her brother. She'd never really put her thoughts about the Goddess into words before, and now that she had she realized that it was harder to do than she'd thought. She wondered if Kyle had any understanding of what she was talking about.

"It's almost like a beehive," he said carefully. "There's this one big queen bee and she sends out the other bees to do stuff."

"Kind of," Kate answered. "But she's not bossy or anything. And really they're all just parts of her. It's not like they work for her or anything like that."

"Okay," Kyle said. "I think I understand that part. But I still don't get what witches *do*. I mean, what's with the chanting and the black robes and all of that?"

"Not everyone wears black robes," Kate said. "That's another one of those things that people just assume. Not that we can't wear them if we want to, but they're just costumes. Witchcraft isn't about what you wear; it's about what you do."

"Which is what I've been trying to get out of you," said Kyle impatiently.

"I know, I know," Kate said. "It's just kind of hard to put into words."

She changes everything she touches, and everything she touches changes. The words to a familiar Wiccan chant ran through her thoughts like water over stones.

"It's about change," Kate said, suddenly understanding how to explain it to Kyle. "Wicca is about change. We try to connect with nature, and with energy, in order to change things."

"What kinds of things?" her brother pressed her.

"Lots of things," Kate said. "The way we see things. The way we interact with people. The way we live. Take Aunt Netty, for example. Remember when we did that healing ritual for her in the hospital?"

Kyle nodded. He'd been there when some of Kate's Wiccan friends had performed a healing circle to try to help her aunt in her fight against cancer. He hadn't known that's what they were doing, exactly, but he'd experienced it. And he'd seen her get better. But Kate knew that, like her father, Kyle attributed Netty's recovery to medicine, not to magic.

"We were trying to get her body to change the way it interacted with the cancer inside of her," Kate said. "We were using the energy within us to help her do that."

Kyle looked skeptical. "And that's what Wicca is?" he said.

"Not entirely," said Kate. "Basically it's about connecting to nature, and to the energy in nature, and finding ways to use those connections to make positive changes in our lives." She'd never summed witchcraft up so simply before, but listening to herself speak, she realized that her definition was pretty accurate.

"So the robes and the candles and the mumbo jumbo . . ." said Kyle, looking at her questioningly.

"Just part of the act," said Kate. "We're a creative bunch."

"I see," said Kyle, nodding.

When he didn't say anything else Kate grew impatient. She wanted some kind of reaction from her brother. She'd gone to a lot of trouble to talk to him, and he wasn't saying anything. Finally she couldn't stand it anymore. "Well?" she demanded.

"Well what?" asked Kyle.

"What do you think?" Kate said.

"I don't know," Kyle said. "I guess I understand it all a little better, but I still think it's kind of woo-woo."

Kate sighed. "Gee, thanks a—"

"Hold on," Kyle said. "Let me finish."

Kate stopped and looked at him. Kyle waited, making sure she wasn't going to interrupt him. Then he continued. "As I was saying, I still think it's kind of woo-woo," he said as Kate made a face. "But if it's important to you, I'm sorry I made you feel bad about it. You're right. I should have listened."

Kate smiled a little. "Thanks," she said. Inside she was jumping for joy. She'd gotten her brother—the most stubborn guy on earth—to admit that he'd been wrong. Maybe he didn't think Wicca was the real thing, but at least he'd listened to her, and at least she'd been able to explain the Craft to him in her own clumsy way.

"So, if I remember correctly this all started because you wanted me to help you get Mom and Dad to let you start seeing Tyler again," Kyle said. "Still need help with that?"

Kate groaned. "No," she said. "But that's a whole other story."

"So tell me," Kyle said. "You're on a roll."

Kate hesitated. Did she want to get into the whole Tyler-and-Annie disaster with Kyle? She'd always been able to talk to him about her problems before, but she was unsure. Part of her wanted to feel as close to him as she used to, to be his little sister. But the way he'd reacted to her at Thanksgiving still bothered her.

She changes everything she touches. The words came to her again. Had she, with the help of the Goddess, really changed the way Kyle thought about Wicca? She didn't know. But she thought that maybe she had, if just a little bit. And he was the one who had suggested talking about Tyler. Maybe it was time to take another chance.

"Okay," she said. "But *this* talk definitely requires cheesecake."

Kyle looked at her in mock terror. "I don't know," he said. "Look what happened last time."

"Don't worry," Kate said, ruffling her brother's hair as she walked out of the room. "I won't tell her about the pierced nipple."

"How did you know?" Kyle called out, running after her.

CHAPTER 8

Cooper stopped running and bent over, her hands on her knees. Her breathing was ragged and she was sure she could taste blood in her mouth. *It's okay*, she told herself. *You're probably just having a heart attack.*

She'd just finished running a mile, and she wanted to die. It hadn't seemed like a very long distance when she'd started out twelve minutes before, but after only a few blocks she'd had second thoughts about her resolution to start exercising. Where was that "runner's high" she'd heard so much about? Where was the thrill of being out in nature? Where was the joy of connecting with her body?

"I've felt better while throwing up," she remarked out loud as she walked around a little, trying to get rid of the persistent cramp in her side. She felt terrible. To make things worse, the batteries on her tape player had run out five minutes into her run, Steven Tyler's voice slurring to a dead stop, and she'd been forced to go the rest of the way without any musical encouragement. And now it had started to rain, a cold winter drizzle that trickled down her neck and made her shiver.

"You're not making this any more appealing," she said, looking up at the sky. Then she turned and ran for home, reaching the front door just as the rain began to fall in earnest.

"How was your run?" her mother asked as Cooper shut the door behind her. Mrs. Rivers was standing in the doorway of the living room.

"Next time I announce that I'm going to engage in physical exercise, stop me," Cooper replied.

Her mother laughed a little too hard. *It's not that funny*, Cooper thought dully as she ran up the stairs to her room.

She put her tape player on the dresser and slipped off her sneakers. Her socks were damp, and her feet felt frozen. She couldn't wait to take a hot shower. Quickly, she removed her clothes and grabbed some jeans and a shirt, which she carried with her to the bathroom.

The hot water felt wonderful when she slipped into the shower. It ran over her shoulders and down her back, warming her skin and making her feel better almost instantly. The steam rose up around her, and she relaxed as her tired muscles were soothed by the warmth. Already she was forgetting about how awful running the mile had been, and part of her even looked forward to doing it again.

It was Wednesday evening. Her homework was

done, and she was looking forward to relaxing with a book for a couple of hours. Friday was right around the corner, and then there was the weekend to look forward to. Kate's birthday party was on Saturday, and that was going to be fun.

You didn't invite Jane yet. The thought slashed across her happiness like a lightning bolt. She'd been avoiding thinking about Jane. When was it that they'd had their falling out? *Monday*, she thought. Only two days. But somehow it seemed longer than that. She'd successfully managed not to think about it too much, and she realized now that part of her had become convinced that the problem was taking care of itself while she was avoiding it. But of course it wasn't, and now she had to decide how she was going to handle things.

But first she was going to wash her hair. The temporary dye she'd put in for New Year's had pretty much worn off, although she noticed that the water streaming around her feet had a faintly pinkish cast to it. *Sort of like the blood going down the drain in the shower scene from* Psycho, she thought with some measure of macabre satisfaction.

Squeezing a little bit of shampoo into her palm, she worked it into her hair. It felt good to be rubbing her scalp. There was something comforting about being in the shower, about being contained in the shell of warmth and steam. She knew her problems—her mother and Jane and the questions about her future with T.J.—were waiting for her outside the shower curtain, ready to sweep over her like a cold wind when she got out, but for now she was happy. For the next five minutes she was going to enjoy being alone with the water.

She rinsed her hair, the water flowing over her face and down her body. It felt great to be clean, and warm, and she was ready to make some decisions. *First I'm going to call Jane*, she told herself. She knew it might be awkward, even painful, but she had to do it. Jane was her friend, after all. Cooper would apologize for telling her friends Jane's secret. She would invite her to Kate's party. Maybe Jane would come; maybe she wouldn't. But at least they'd be talking again.

Cooper turned off the water and pushed the curtain aside. She'd left the bathroom door closed so that the steam would stay inside, and it filled the small space with its ghostly fog. She grabbed her towel from the hook by the shower and dried herself off. Then she pulled on her clothes and opened the door.

She walked quickly to her room, not wanting to stay in the drafty hallway any longer than she had to. As she passed the stairway she heard music coming from downstairs. Her mother had put something on the CD player. What was it? Cooper paused and strained to hear. She could just make out the sound of someone singing. *Joni Mitchell*, she thought as she made out the words. *She must really be depressed.*

She continued on into her room, shutting the

door to drown out the sound of the music. She wished she could make her mother feel better. More and more she had been having a drink or two after dinner and listening to sad music. Cooper wanted to talk to her about how she was feeling, but she couldn't. She and her mother had never been very close. Besides, she was the daughter. Her mother was supposed to comfort *her*. Cooper didn't know what to do. She made a mental note to talk to her father about it the next time he called. *But first things first*, she thought as she picked up her phone and dialed Jane's number. She would get their conversation out of the way so she could enjoy the rest of her evening.

The phone rang three, four times, then five, with no answer. Jane always picked up before three rings, and Cooper was about to hang up when she heard the sound of someone fumbling with the receiver.

"Hello?" said a soft voice, almost like a child.

"Mr. Goldstein?" Cooper said, surprised. Jane's grandfather never answered the phone. Jane had told her once that he was almost mortally afraid of it and its ringing, one of the many eccentricities he'd developed in his old age.

"Yes," the old man said. "Who is this?"

"It's Cooper, Mr. Goldstein," said Cooper. "Jane's friend," she added, thinking he might not remember her name.

"Oh," he said. "Yes."

"Is Jane home?" asked Cooper, still unsure of whether or not Mr. Goldstein had any idea who she was.

"No," he said. "No, she's not."

"Do you have any idea when she'll be back?" asked Cooper.

"You're Jane's friend," he said. "Cooper?"

"That's right," Cooper answered. "I come over to play music with Jane sometimes."

"Ah, yes," said the old man. "I like you."

Cooper smiled to herself. "I like you, too, Mr. Goldstein," she said. "Do you know when Jane will be back?"

Mr. Goldstein sighed. "She's not here," he said.

Cooper wasn't sure what to say. Jane's grandfather seemed to be a little out of it, and she didn't want to confuse him any more than he already was. She was just about to say that she would call back later when Mr. Goldstein said, "She's at the hospital."

"Hospital?" Cooper said, worried. "Is everything okay?"

"They took her there," said Mr. Goldstein, ignoring Cooper's question.

"Who?" Cooper said. "Who took her there? And why?"

"I don't know," answered the old man, sounding very sad.

Don't know who or don't know why? Cooper thought impatiently. She took a breath to calm herself before speaking again.

"Is Jane in the hospital?" she asked.

"Yes," said Mr. Goldstein.

Cooper knew that asking what had happened would probably be too much for him, so she decided to try a different approach. "Which hospital?" she asked. "Do you know which one?"

There was silence on the other end. Then, just as Cooper thought she would scream with frustration, Mr. Goldstein said, "Saint Andrew's." He sounded as if he'd just remembered his own name and was very pleased about it.

"Thank you," Cooper said. "I have to go now, Mr. Goldstein. But thank you for telling me."

"You're welcome," Mr. Goldstein said. "Goodbye."

He hung up. Cooper sat for a moment, holding the phone, until she heard the dial tone buzzing to remind her that she hadn't hung up. She set the phone down and tried to think. Jane was in the hospital. Why? What had happened? And who was taking care of Mr. Goldstein?

She pulled on socks and shoes and looked for her jacket. She had to get to St. Andrew's. But suddenly it was like she couldn't find anything she needed. Her car keys weren't where they usually were on her desk. She couldn't find her wallet. She turned around and around, thinking a million different things. Finally she had to force herself to stop and breathe. She stayed completely still for a minute, until her heart stopped racing and she could think clearly. Then she opened her eyes and found everything she needed. Moments later she was running out the door.

"I have to go out," she called to her mother, who responded with something Cooper couldn't hear. Mrs. Rivers had turned up the volume on the stereo, and Joni Mitchell filled the living room with her plaintive voice as Cooper left the house.

She got into her car and drove as quickly as she could to the hospital. *Please let Jane be all right*, she thought as she waited at a red light. *Please let Jane be all right*. She had no idea what had happened to her, but she couldn't help thinking the worst, and she didn't want anything to happen before she could see her friend.

Finally she reached the hospital, where she parked in the first empty spot and ran inside to the reception desk. The woman sitting there smiled kindly at her. "Can I help you?" she asked.

"I'm looking for a friend of mine," Cooper said. "Jane Goldstein. I'm not sure when she came in. I just found out that she's here."

The woman typed something into her computer and peered at her screen. "She's on the third floor," she said. "Room three twenty-seven."

"Thanks," said Cooper. She turned and walked to the bank of elevators, pressing the up button and waiting impatiently for the car to arrive. When it did she got inside and pushed the button for the third floor.

As the elevator went up Cooper scanned the directory posted on the wall. What was on the third floor anyway? Cooper looked, praying that she wouldn't discover that Jane was on the cancer ward or in some other equally distressing unit. "Psychiatry," she read with some surprise. Why would Jane be there?

Before she had time to think about it the doors opened and she stepped out. She glanced to the left and right and then followed the arrow pointing to rooms 301 to 345. Room 327 was at the end of the hall. Cooper approached the door nervously, wondering what she would find waiting for her.

When she looked inside, she saw Jane sitting up in bed, looking very unhappy. A dark-haired woman was sitting in a chair at the end of the bed, looking equally unhappy, and a man was standing beside Jane. He, too, had dark hair, with a thinning patch at the back of his head. He was staring out the window, his hands on his hips.

Cooper wasn't sure what she should do. She wanted to say something, but nothing came to mind. Finally she cleared her throat. The man turned around. When he saw her, he frowned.

"I suppose this is her," he said, looking at Jane.

Jane glanced up. When she saw Cooper, she closed her eyes, as if trying to block out the sight. "No," she said. "That's not her."

"Then who are you?" the man asked, turning

around to face Cooper.

Cooper didn't like the way he was speaking to her, and she felt anger rising up through her worry. Now that she saw that Jane seemed to be okay, she was able to think about other things. She looked the man in the eye and said, "I'm her friend, Cooper. Who are you?"

The man seemed taken aback. He blinked once or twice before answering, "I'm her father."

It was Cooper's turn to blink. She'd never met Jane's parents. She looked at Mr. Goldstein, then at the woman in the chair, who she guessed was Mrs. Goldstein. The woman smiled faintly, then looked away. *She's pretty*, Cooper thought distractedly. *Jane looks a lot like her*.

"Are you one of the people she met at that place?" Mr. Goldstein demanded.

"What place?" Cooper asked, not understanding.

"Cooper doesn't go to the center," Jane said weakly.

Suddenly, Cooper understood what Mr. Goldstein was asking her. But she still didn't understand what was going on.

"Are you okay?" she asked, addressing her question to Jane.

"No, she's not okay," said Mr. Goldstein. "She tried to kill herself."

"What?" Cooper said, alarmed.

Jane looked away.

"Tell her," Mr. Goldstein said. "Tell your friend

what you did." He turned back to Cooper, his eyes flashing angrily. "My daughter took some of her grandfather's sedatives," he said, as if he were a news anchor announcing a breaking story.

"David," Mrs. Goldstein said quietly.

"What?" said Jane's father. "Ruth, our daughter tried to kill herself."

Mrs. Goldstein looked at Cooper helplessly.

"I think I should go," Cooper said. Then she looked at Jane. "Call me when you can," she said, not sure what else she could say.

Jane looked at her. She didn't say anything, but she nodded slightly. Cooper smiled at her friend. "Blessed be," she said, knowing Jane would understand.

She turned and walked out of the room without saying anything to Mr. and Mrs. Goldstein. She'd gotten halfway to the elevators when she heard someone following her. A moment later Mrs. Goldstein appeared at her side.

"I'm sorry about my husband," she said. "He's upset, as you can imagine."

"I imagine Jane is more upset," said Cooper coolly.

Mrs. Goldstein closed her eyes. When she opened them again, Cooper saw tears. "It's like we don't even know who she is," she said. "We're gone so much and—" She stopped, breathing deeply, as if to keep from sobbing.

"What happened?" Cooper asked her.

"We came home late Tuesday night," Mrs. Goldstein said. "When I knocked on her door there was no answer, so I went in. She was on the bed. I thought she was asleep. Then I realized that she was still dressed. And when I tried to wake her, she wouldn't open her eyes."

Jane's mother put her hand to her head. "Then I saw the note," she said.

"Note?" asked Cooper.

Mrs. Goldstein reached into her pocket and pulled out a crumpled piece of paper. She handed it to Cooper, who smoothed it out and read it.

Mom and Dad:
I know you won't understand this, so I just want to
tell you that it isn't your fault. I just don't know what
else to do. Everything hurts right now, and I just
want it to stop. I'm sorry if I'm disappointing you.
I love you very much.
Jane

"She had taken a handful of her grandfather's pills," Mrs. Goldstein said, looking as if she was remembering the scene in her head. "When I felt her chest and realized she was still alive, I was so relieved I thought maybe she was playing a joke on us. But she just wouldn't wake up. We called the paramedics, and they brought her here."

Cooper kept looking at Jane's note. She couldn't believe that her friend had tried to kill herself. *Was it because of what I did?* she wondered. She couldn't help but ask herself that question. After all, Jane had been really upset with her.

"Are you and my daughter close?" asked Mrs. Goldstein.

Cooper nodded. "We play music together," she said. "But we sort of had a falling out recently. I betrayed her trust," she explained, not sure why she was confessing her indiscretion to Jane's mother. "I called tonight to apologize, and that's when I found out she was here."

Mrs. Goldstein nodded. "She told us that she's—" she said, unable to finish the sentence.

"A lesbian?" said Cooper. "I know. She told me, too. I guess that's what this is all about."

"My husband is so angry," said Jane's mother. "I know it's more that he's scared, that he thought we might really lose her. But he can't admit that."

"Is there anything I can do?" asked Cooper. She had no idea how she might be able to help, or even if the Goldsteins wanted her around their daughter—but it seemed the right thing to say.

"Jane doesn't have a lot of friends," answered Mrs. Goldstein. "She needs the ones she's got."

Cooper smiled. "I think I can do that," she said.

Mrs. Goldstein smiled back, looking a little more relaxed. "Thank you," she said.

Cooper nodded. "Do you mind if I come see her?" she asked.

"I think she'll be home on Friday," answered

Jane's mother. "Why don't you stop by then? I'm sure she'll be happy to see you."

I don't know about that, Cooper thought, but what she said was, "I'll stop by after school."

CHAPTER 9

"Hey, sis."

Annie laughed at Becka's greeting when she answered the phone. "I was just thinking about you," she said.

"Nothing bad, I hope," said Becka.

"No," Annie replied. "Nothing bad. I was just thinking about what it will be like to have someone my own age around all the time. I think Meg is getting worried that we're going to gang up on her or something."

"I'm the one who should be worried," said Becka. "I've never had sisters before."

"Well, technically we won't be sisters," Annie said thoughtfully. "Sarah's my aunt, so that makes us more like stepcousins."

"I like sisters better," said Becka.

"Me, too," said Annie. "But either way, it will be cool."

"Can you believe this is really happening?" Becka said more seriously. "I mean, it was what—

less than three months ago that I found you outside our house?"

"The two of them move fast," Annie agreed. "I guess when you know, you know."

"My dad has been impossible ever since he got back," said Becka. "It's like he's sixteen again or something. He can't concentrate on anything, and he's always smiling."

"Aunt Sarah is the same way," said Annie. "Yesterday she left a bagel in the toaster so long it burned and the smoke detector went off."

Annie hesitated. There was something she had been wondering about, and she wasn't sure if she should bring it up. But she thought she knew Becka well enough, so she said, "Does it bother you at all? I mean the fact that your dad is getting remarried?"

She could hear Becka breathe in on the other end. "I was a baby when my mother died," she said. "I never really knew her. But I've grown up with pictures of her all over the house, and with hearing the stories my dad told me about her. I feel like I really did know her. And yeah, it's kind of weird to think of him feeling the way about someone else that I know he felt about her. But your aunt is great, and I know she makes my dad really happy. That's what matters."

"Sometimes I forget that Aunt Sarah isn't my mom," said Annie. "I think Meg probably really does feel like Sarah's her mother, because Meg was just a baby when our parents died. Sometimes when

I think about her marrying your dad, I wonder if I'll feel like I have a father again."

"It's like we're each getting the part that we lost when we were little," Becka said.

Annie thought back to Samhain, when she'd had a chance to say good-bye to her parents' ghosts. She'd known then that she was letting go of a part of her that she'd been hanging on to, a part that needed to be set free. Now she was getting another part back. She was going to be part of a larger family, one that had been brought together, in a way, by her parents' deaths. Would they approve? she wondered. Would they be happy for Aunt Sarah, and for her and Meg?

"Has your father talked to you about the whole moving thing?" Annie asked Becka.

"Not really," she answered. "He said that they haven't decided anything." She paused. "What do you hope they do?"

This was another topic Annie had been reluctant to bring up, but now that Becka had, she figured she might as well tell the truth. "I hope we stay here," she said. "I really love this house and my friends."

Becka sighed. "I know," she said. "I love this house, too, and my friends here. No matter what happens, it's going to be hard on one of us."

"How about this?" Annie said. "Whoever has to move gets control of the television viewing choices for three months."

"Nice idea," Becka said. "But neither one of us

watches television. How about whoever moves gets first bathroom usage in the mornings for six months?"

"You mean there might be *bathroom sharing?*" Annie said, pretending to be horrified. "No one mentioned that!"

"Now things don't look so great, do they?" said Becka.

Annie laughed. "I think sharing a bathroom is worth getting a cool new sister," she said.

"Yeah," said Becka. "You're right. But the first time you leave the top off the toothpaste, it's *over.*"

"I'll keep that in mind," Annie said.

They talked for another few minutes and then Annie hung up. After she put the phone down, she lay on her bed, thinking about the conversation she'd just had. What *would* it be like living with Becka? she wondered. It had always been just her and Meg. What would happen when Becka became part of the family? She really liked Becka, but would they still get along when they had to spend every day together? She liked Cooper and Kate, too, but she had a hard time imagining what it would be like having one of them around all the time.

Where will we put everyone if they move here? she thought suddenly. Grayson, obviously, would sleep in Aunt Sarah's room. But what about Becka? There was another bedroom next to Meg's, but it was filled with a lot of things they didn't really have places for anywhere else. *Besides,* Annie thought,

Grayson will need a room to write in.

That meant that the only other room was on the third floor, across from hers. Would she and Becka share the floor? She looked around. She loved her room. She loved being on the third floor. She particularly liked that she had it all to herself. It was the one place she could go where no one else was allowed unless she invited them there. The thought that she might have to share it with someone else really upset her.

She felt guilty about that. She liked Becka. But she didn't want to share a floor with her. Was Becka worried about the same thing? Annie thought about the house in San Francisco. It was smaller than this one. If they moved there, she would definitely be sharing a room with Becka, or even Meg. She was certain that the thought had crossed Becka's mind as well. How could it not? And if Becka felt like she did, then Annie felt terrible about maybe being the one to move in and force her to share her space.

She didn't want to think about it anymore. She was sure everything would be fine, and worrying wasn't going to help. She needed something to distract herself with. But what? For once, she didn't feel like reading. She glanced out the window and saw that it was still raining, as it had been since the day before. *So much for taking a walk*, she thought.

Why don't you do a ritual? The question popped into her mind unbidden. But once it was there, it made perfect sense. She hadn't done a ritual in quite a while, and she realized that she missed doing them. But what kind should she do? She didn't feel like doing a plain old meditation exercise, nor did she want to do something like work with Tarot cards or anything like that. She wanted to do something different.

She thought for a while, running through the different kinds of rituals she could think of. *Think of something you want to achieve*, she told herself. After all, the whole point of doing a ritual was to make something happen. What did she want to have happen? She thought some more, but she was feeling totally uninspired. The grayness of the weather, and the coldness of the time of year, had left her feeling tired and totally uncreative.

That's it! she thought. She could do a ritual to inspire herself. She'd never done one before. It would be fun, and it would be a great way to practice some of her ritual-creating skills.

She got up, filled with a new sense of purpose, and started gathering things together. She looked around her room, trying to decide what would work in the ritual she wanted to do. She immediately thought of candles. Luckily, she had just bought some at Crones' Circle. They were small red ones. She'd liked the color, so bright and cheerful amidst the coldness of winter, and she'd bought twelve of them without knowing exactly what she was going to do with them. Now she got the bag containing them from her closet and placed it on the floor.

What else? It occurred to her that she wanted to invoke a goddess of some kind, someone to help inspire her. Who would be good? She considered and rejected several candidates before the name of Brigid came to her. That was perfect. Brigid was the Celtic goddess of inspiration. And Annie had just the thing to use in a ritual involving Brigid, a small three-legged cauldron like the kind Brigid was supposed to have possessed. She got it and placed it beside the candles.

Now that she had the tools, she had to decide what to do with them. She took the cauldron and put it in the center of what was going to be her magic circle. Then she placed the red candles all around it, marking the perimeter of the circle. After that she gathered some things from her altar, and it was time to begin the ritual. While there were things she was still unsure of, she decided that she would make them up as she went along. One thing she'd learned during her nine months of studying Wicca was that sometimes the best rituals weren't totally thought out ahead of time. *Besides*, she told herself, *this is supposed to be a ritual to inspire creativity. So be creative!*

She began by turning off the lights, so that the room was shrouded in rainy gray light. Then she slipped out of her clothes and pulled on a white robe that she had made to use in her rituals. It was a simple thing, and Kate had helped her sew it. Annie liked the way it hung around her and made her feel like she was about to do something special.

She only wore the robe for rituals, so that whenever she put it on it helped her get in the mood.

Next she lit the candles around the circle. When it was completed she stood back and looked at it. The tiny flames danced merrily, and she loved the red glow that the candles made. She sniffed the air and realized that they also gave off a faint scent, like cinnamon and roses. It perfumed the room and added to the sense of creativity that was growing with each part of the ritual.

It was time to cast the circle. Annie had been reading about different circle-casting rituals in a book that Archer had loaned her. One of the methods had interested her, and she decided to try it out.

First she picked up the small bowl of salt that she kept on her altar to represent the element of earth. Holding it in her hand, she walked clockwise around the circle of candles, sprinkling a little bit of salt on the floor as she invoked the powers of earth into the circle.

"Circle of earth," she said. "Cleanse and protect this sacred space."

She completed her journey around the circle and placed the bowl of salt on the floor. Then she picked up a feather she'd collected on one of her walks in the woods over the summer. Holding that in her hand, she walked the circle again, this time calling on the element of air.

"Circle of air," she said. "Sweep clean this sacred space."

The third time around she picked up one of the candles from the circle and carried that with her, saying as she went, "Circle of fire, illuminate this sacred space." And on her fourth trip she held in her hand a bowl of water, sprinkling it on the floor while calling out, "Circle of water, bind and close this sacred space."

When she had invoked all four of the elements, she stepped into the circle of candles and stood in the center with her arms held up. It was time for her to call on Brigid and invite her into the circle as well. She paused a moment, grounding herself and letting the power of the circle surround her and fill her.

"Brigid," she said when she felt ready. "Goddess of inspiration. I invite you into my circle tonight and ask you to bless me with your gifts of inspiration and creativity. Be with me now."

She then knelt beside the cauldron that sat in the circle. She had placed a candle inside of it, and now she lit it. The cauldron seemed to be filled with fire, just as she imagined Brigid's cauldron of inspiration would be. As she gazed at it, she imagined that the flames were the sparks of ideas, dancing wildly as they flew about inside the cauldron.

She wasn't exactly sure what to do next. She'd only thought as far as casting the circle and invoking Brigid. That had all gone really well, but now she was unsure of herself. What was she supposed to do? For a moment she panicked, thinking that she had done something wrong.

She decided to just relax. She thought that if maybe she sat quietly then an idea would come to her. So she stayed where she was, staring into the depths of the cauldron at the flame. She watched it moving, the colors shifting against one another as it flickered. And soon she began to see an image in her mind.

She was walking on a path that led to a little cottage in a field. It was nighttime, and there were no lights except for the stars and a warm light that spilled out of the windows of the cottage. Annie stopped outside of it and peered inside. There she saw a woman standing in front of a cauldron. She had long auburn hair, and she wore a red dress. Annie knew instantly that it was Brigid.

The woman turned and looked at her. "Come in," she said, her voice like honey. "You are welcome in my house."

Annie entered the door of the cottage and stepped inside the room where the woman stood. Brigid beckoned her closer, and Annie went to stand beside her. Brigid turned and pointed into the cauldron. "Look inside," she said.

Annie bent and looked into the cauldron. It was filled with the brightest light she'd ever seen. It glowed with an intensity so fierce that she feared being burned by it, even though it gave off no heat and didn't hurt her eyes. It seemed almost alive, rolling around on itself as if it was playing, or dancing.

"Go ahead," Brigid urged her. "Reach inside.

Take some for yourself."

Annie looked into the goddess's face. "I'm afraid," she said.

"Don't fear it," Brigid told her. "Be brave."

Annie looked again into the cauldron. She *was* afraid. But she also wanted to accept Brigid's gift. Finally she reached out and tentatively lowered her hands toward the light, cupping them together. Still expecting to feel her skin burn, she plunged them into the flames.

She wasn't burned. Instead, she felt more alive than she'd ever felt before. The light clung to her, filling her cupped hands. She lifted them and saw it pooled in her fingers, still moving. She lifted her hands over her head and opened them, letting the light fall over her. She felt it trickle over her head and down her body. Where it touched her she felt tiny sparks on her skin, like she was being washed in electricity. It left her feeling excited and filled with the desire to do something, to dance, or to sing.

Or paint, she thought suddenly. She looked around and saw that she was still sitting in her own circle. Her hands were over her head, and she was looking down at her little cauldron, where the candle still burned.

It felt so real, she thought. For a minute she really had believed that she was in Brigid's house. *And maybe I was*, she told herself. After all, she was working magic, and magic could do all kinds of things. That was the beauty of doing a ritual.

Then she remembered her thought about painting. Where had that come from? *Your resolution*, she reminded herself. That was it. She had wanted to spend more time with her painting.

She looked around and spied the painting sitting on the easel by the window. It was one she'd begun a few days before. She'd worked on it for a while and then left it, unsure of where it was going. It was unlike anything else she'd ever done—an abstract piece made up of different shades of red against a black background. When she'd started it, she'd just been playing around. There hadn't been any particular image in her mind; she'd just been painting.

But now she knew what it was she'd been working on. The red paint reminded her of the fire in Brigid's cauldron, burning brightly against a black sky. Looking at it, she had an idea for how to finish it. And she also knew what she was going to do with it when it was done.

CHAPTER 10

On Friday night Cooper went to see Jane. Standing outside the Goldsteins' door, she almost turned around and went home. All she could picture in her mind was the way Jane's father had glared at her in the hospital. Would he be there, and would he look at her the same way this time?

He's just scared for his daughter, she told herself repeatedly as she knocked.

Mrs. Goldstein opened the door. When she saw Cooper she smiled. "Thank you for coming by," she said as she stepped aside and Cooper entered the house. Jane's mother shut the door and turned to Cooper. "She came home this afternoon," she said. "I know she'll be happy to see a familiar face. I think she was getting tired of only being around her father and me."

"Is she in her room?" Cooper asked. She hadn't seen any sign of Mr. Goldstein, and she wanted to avoid him if at all possible.

Mrs. Goldstein nodded. "Go on in," she said.

Cooper walked down the hallway to Jane's door. It was shut, so she knocked. When there was no answer she opened the door and looked in. Jane was propped up in bed, her head on the pillow and her eyes closed. Cooper thought she was asleep, and she started to shut the door again. But then Jane opened her eyes.

"Oh, it's you," she said. "Come in."

Cooper went in and shut the door behind her. Jane sat up.

"I was just pretending to be asleep," she said. "My mother keeps coming in to see if I want anything, and it's making me nuts."

Cooper laughed. "Good move," she said, happy to see that Jane at least *sounded* like she was back to her old self. She handed Jane the bag she'd brought with her. "For you," she said.

Jane took the bag and raised an eyebrow. "Dare I look inside?" she asked. "It's not a fuzzy pink teddy bear, is it? I'd have to be sick."

"You'll just have to look," said Cooper, pulling up a chair and sitting down.

Jane opened the bag tentatively and peered inside. Then she reached in and pulled out some comic books. "*Industrial Mermaid* and *Banshee*," she said approvingly. "Very cool."

"There's more," Cooper said, sending Jane back into the bag. This time she pulled out two CDs and several candy bars.

"I figured everyone needs Patsy Cline, AC/DC,

and chocolate when they're laid up," said Cooper.

Jane looked at her, grinning. "You're the best," she said. "Thanks."

There was an awkward silence as the two of them looked away and didn't speak. Jane put Cooper's gifts to the side and sat with her hands on her lap, nervously rubbing her fingers together. Cooper pretended to be engrossed in pulling a stray thread from her shirt.

"I'm sorry I freaked you out," Jane said finally.

Cooper stopped playing with the thread and rubbed her nose. "I'm sorry I told Annie and Kate about you," she said.

"And Sasha," added Jane.

"And Sasha," echoed Cooper, rolling her eyes. "Man, do you ever hold a grudge." She looked at Jane. "Did you do it because of me telling them?" she asked. It was the question that had been weighing on her mind ever since she'd heard that Jane had tried to kill herself.

"No," Jane said, and Cooper felt something in her chest release like a balloon being set free. "And to tell the truth, I wasn't really trying to kill myself. I knew I didn't take enough pills for that."

"Then what was it?" asked Cooper, not understanding.

Jane sighed. "It was more like I wanted to kill myself, but I knew I would never do that, so I did the next best thing."

"To tell the truth," said Cooper, "it did seem

kind of unlike you. I mean, you're one of the toughest people I know."

"Do you really think so?" Jane asked, sounding truly surprised to hear Cooper say that.

Cooper nodded. "Definitely," she said.

"I don't always feel that way," Jane said. "I mean, I try to be. Sometimes I think I try too hard, you know? I keep people away because I don't want to give them the chance to hurt me. When I let Max in, it was a big deal. Then when she . . . did what she did, I felt like a fool. I felt like I'd stood in front of the whole world and had my pants fall down. And worse," she added. "Not only did my pants fall down, but I was wearing panties with little *flowers* on them."

Cooper couldn't help but laugh. "You're too much," she said. "And I know what you mean. I felt like that when I said yes to going out with T.J. You don't know how close I came to telling him I wouldn't."

Jane nodded. "That's how it was with Max," she said. "And then, when she broke up with me, it was like every fear I'd ever had was confirmed. I told myself that I'd never let anyone do that again, even though, when I really think about it, I want someone to ask me out again."

"Someone will," Cooper said. "Someone better than Max."

"Maybe," Jane said. "Anyway, I just didn't want to be here anymore. And then when you told me about telling the girls, all I could think about was that now everyone would be talking about it."

"So it *was* because of me," Cooper said, suddenly feeling terrible again.

"No," Jane said. "No, it really wasn't. It was just that I've kept this to myself for so long, and suddenly it was out in the open. I couldn't take it back. And that made me think about telling my parents and my sisters and—"

She stopped, looking down at her hands. She sat that way for a minute, then resumed speaking. "Did you know that during the Holocaust the Nazis put gay people in the concentration camps?" she said.

"No," said Cooper. "I didn't know that."

"Hitler believed that they were a threat to the pure race," Jane continued. "He made them wear pink triangles on their clothes. If they were Jewish they had to wear the Star of David and the triangle, but the triangle was considered more shameful. No one really talks about that when they talk about the Holocaust. No one talks about their relatives who were killed because they had pink triangles on their clothes."

Jane had begun to cry. Tears slipped down her cheeks and fell quietly onto the bed. She didn't make any move to wipe them away. "I kept thinking about that," she said. "And it made me really sad."

Cooper moved to the bed. She put her arms around her friend. Jane hugged her back. "I didn't know how to tell them," she said, and Cooper knew that she was talking about her family.

They sat that way for a while, Cooper rubbing Jane's back while Jane let out her emotions. Then Jane sat back and wiped her eyes. "I knew they were coming back," she said. "I knew they'd find me. I thought if they were worried about me it might make telling them easier." She sniffed. "Pathetic, huh?"

"No," Cooper said, shaking her head. "Sometimes it's easier to be a drama queen than it is to just talk. I know how that is."

Jane gave a half laugh, half sob. "You?" she said. "I can't even *imagine*."

Cooper gave her a warning look. "Don't start with me," she said. "I'll take those comic books right back."

There was a knock on the door and Mrs. Goldstein looked in. "Everything okay?" she asked. "Do you need anything?"

"I'm fine," Jane said. "Thanks."

"Okay," her mother said. "You just call me if you want anything."

She shut the door. Jane sighed. "Well, I got their attention, all right. I think maybe I overdid it."

"I take it from your father's reaction in the hospital that things did not go well," said Cooper.

"Not exactly," Jane replied. "I'd say his reaction was somewhere in between the way he reacted when my sister totaled the car and when Bush was elected president."

"Yikes," Cooper said. "That must have been tough."

Jane shrugged. "It was about what I expected," she said. "My parents are your all-too-typical upper-middle-class liberals—they're very open-minded when it comes to *other* people, but when it comes to their own families they don't always cope well."

"How are they treating you?" asked Cooper.

"Well, my father has gone off on another business trip," answered Jane. "That's his way of dealing with it. And my mother, as you can see, has become Nurse Jane Fuzzywuzzy. She's resorting to the old Jewish standby of trying to fix everything with chicken soup. Which, by the way, she can't make at *all*."

"And your sisters?" asked Cooper.

"They haven't told them, of course," Jane told her. "I think they're hoping that this was a onetime thing and now I'm over it."

"It *was* a onetime thing, wasn't it?" Cooper asked, concerned.

"Oh, the pill thing was," said Jane, waving her hand at Cooper. "I'm talking about the whole lesbian thing."

"Ah," Cooper said, understanding. "What do you think is going to happen there?"

Jane shook her head and let out a puff of air. "Who can say?" she said. "Probably we won't talk about it."

"Are you okay with that?" asked Cooper.

"Yes and no," answered Jane. "I don't think I

would want to talk to them about my personal life even if I was dating guys, so on that level I don't care. But I do want them to know who I am. I don't want to have to hide it from them. And I'm not going to. I'm still going to go to the center. I'm still going to have the same friends."

"What if they tell you you can't go?" Cooper said.

"They're never here," Jane said. "How will they know? Besides, I think they'll calm down. My father just needed to blow off steam. I think he feels guilty about being away so much."

"What did your grandfather say?" Cooper asked. She hadn't seen old Mr. Goldstein when she came in, and she wondered how he had reacted to his granddaughter's hospitalization.

"They told him that I had an allergic reaction to something I ate," Jane said. "Of course they think he can't handle the truth. I mean, the man was in a *concentration camp* for two years and survived, but they want to protect him. They don't know him any more than they know me."

"I think there's going to be a lot of talking going on around here in the next couple of weeks," remarked Cooper thoughtfully.

Jane groaned. "Please," she said. "No more talking. I just want to go back to being little old antisocial me."

"I think you're on your way," Cooper joked.

"So, does this mean our band is still on?"

"Most definitely," Jane said. "Are you kidding? With all of this new material to write about, I'll be piling up songs left and right."

Cooper laughed. Then she cleared her throat. "I know we joke about a lot of things," she said seriously. "But I want you to know that you really scared me there. And I also want you to know that you can talk to me about anything." She cracked a smile. "And next time I won't tell my friends about it."

Jane nodded. "I'm sorry I scared you," she said. "And it's okay about telling your friends. I think I'm glad that they know. And I *know* that I'm glad that I can talk to you. I haven't had a real friend like you in a long, long time."

There was another knock on the door and Mrs. Goldstein looked in again. This time she was carrying a tray. "Dinner," she said. "Chicken soup."

Jane and Cooper looked at each other and laughed. "I should go," Cooper said. "But hey, we're having a birthday party for Kate tomorrow. It's at Annie's house. If you feel up to it, we'd love to have you come."

Jane looked at her mother. "Is that okay?" she asked.

Mrs. Goldstein put the tray on Jane's desk. She looked at Cooper, and seemed to be thinking about something. Then she nodded. "I think that would be all right," she said.

"Great," said Cooper cheerfully. "I'll write down the address."

She got a piece of paper and a pen from Jane's desk and wrote Annie's address on it while Mrs. Goldstein arranged the tray with the soup on it on Jane's lap. Cooper waved the paper at Jane. "Here it is," she said. "The party starts at five. Don't be late."

"I won't," Jane said, looking unhappily at the soup on her tray. "Will there be food?" she asked plaintively. "*Good* food?"

Cooper tried hard not to laugh. "Piles of it," she said. "See you tomorrow."

Jane waved and Cooper left the room, followed by Mrs. Goldstein. Jane's mother walked her to the door, where she paused. "Can I ask you something?" she asked Cooper.

"Sure," Cooper said.

"My daughter," Mrs. Goldstein said uncomfortably. "Is she okay?"

Cooper looked at the woman's anxious face. She tried to imagine what it must be like to be in her position, dealing with something she really didn't understand and being so afraid. Then she thought of her own mother, and how unhappy she seemed to be lately.

"Yes," she said. "Jane is okay. She's a good person, Mrs. Goldstein. Maybe she's a little different—and I don't mean the gay thing, I mean just in general. But she's okay." Cooper paused for a moment, thinking. "My mom would probably ask Jane the same question about me if she could," she added.

Cooper heard Mrs. Goldstein laugh for the first time. She sounded relieved, as if she'd been wanting to laugh for a long time. She put her hand to her forehead. "I worry about her so much," she said. "Sometimes I feel like I'm looking at a stranger."

"She's a great person," said Cooper. "You should get to know her. I think you'd like her."

Jane's mother looked at her, and for a moment Cooper wondered if she'd said too much. Then Mrs. Goldstein shook her head. "I think you're right," she said.

"I'll see Jane tomorrow," Cooper said.

She left the house and drove home. She was glad that she'd been able to talk to Jane, and that they were still friends. And she was glad that she'd been able to talk to Mrs. Goldstein. She seemed like a nice lady, and Cooper hoped that things between her and Jane worked out. As for Mr. Goldstein, he seemed like a bigger challenge. But she had no doubt that her friend would be up to dealing with him.

She looked at her watch. It was almost eight o'clock. She was supposed to meet T.J. for a movie at nine, and she wanted to change first. She drove to her house and went inside. When she opened the front door, she heard the unmistakable sound of Joni Mitchell still playing on the stereo. Had her mother been playing the same CD over and over? Cooper walked into the living room to see.

Her mother was on the couch, stretched out

with one arm hanging over the edge. The glass she'd been drinking from sat on the floor beside her. Cooper surveyed the scene, a sick feeling growing inside of her. Part of her wanted to just go upstairs, change, and go out with T.J. She knew they would have a good time, and she knew it would make her forget about seeing her mother this way.

Then she thought of Jane. She had just told Mrs. Goldstein that she should listen to her daughter and find out who she was. *Maybe you need the same advice*, she thought. Maybe it was time she and her mother *really* talked. Her mother was clearly hurting, and Cooper didn't know what she could do about it. After all, she was the daughter. It wasn't her job to take care of her mother. They'd always pretty much left each other alone, and Cooper had been fine with that.

But she's part of you, she found herself thinking. *You're connected to her, and she's part of your path.* There it was again—her path. Cooper sighed. She knew that everything that happened to her was part of the journey she was on, and that every challenge she faced helped her grow. This was another challenge, and she could either turn her back on it or she could meet it head-on.

She walked to the stereo and turned Joni off. Then she picked up the glass and took it to the kitchen. Picking up the phone, she dialed T.J.'s number.

"Hey," she said when he answered. "Do you mind if we skip the movie tonight?"

"Not if you want to," T.J. answered. "Is every-thing okay?"

"It will be," Cooper said. "I think. Can I call you later?"

"Sure," said her boyfriend. "I'll be up."

"Thanks," Cooper said. "Hey, and guess what?"

"What?"

"I love you," Cooper said.

"That's good," T.J. said, "because I love you, too."

Cooper hung up. Then she filled two fresh glasses with iced tea from the refrigerator and went out to have a talk with her mother.

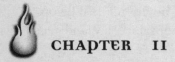

CHAPTER 11

"Happy birthday."

"Thanks," said Kate. "It's not often you get to celebrate your birthday with your therapist."

Dr. Hagen tapped her pencil against the pad in her hand. "How does it feel to be sixteen?" she asked.

Kate shrugged. "Not much different," she said. "I was expecting more."

"Trust me," the doctor said, "once you start hitting the really *big* numbers, you'll feel different."

Kate laughed. It wasn't often that Dr. Hagen let loose and joked around. It made Kate feel almost like they were friends instead of doctor and patient.

"So," Dr. Hagen continued, "what do you want to talk about on this momentous occasion?"

Usually at her Saturday morning therapy sessions Kate felt awkward, like she was being interviewed for a job she was totally unqualified for or being tested on a subject she hadn't studied in enough detail. But today she had something to say.

"I'm really proud of myself," she told Dr. Hagen. "I talked to Kyle about Wicca."

"Really?" said the doctor neutrally. "And how did that go?"

"Better than I thought it would," answered Kate. "At first I got angry with him, and I was just going to forget the whole thing. But then I calmed down and realized that if I can't even explain the Craft to my brother, then I probably don't have any business calling myself an almost-witch."

"And is that what you're calling yourself?" the doctor asked her.

"Yes," Kate said confidently. She'd never really claimed the word *witch* in talking with her therapist—or with anyone, really—and it felt good to do it now. "Yes," she said again. "I'm an almost-witch."

Dr. Hagen wrote something on the pad. "When you came to see me, your parents were worried that you were confused," she said. "They thought you were involved in Wicca because you were feeling alienated. Why do you think you're involved in it?"

Kate didn't answer for a minute. She thought about the doctor's question. Why *was* she involved in Wicca? It took some time for her to organize her thoughts.

"At first I think maybe I did do it because I felt alienated," said Kate. "I knew I didn't want to be like Sherrie and some of the other people I was hanging out with, and being into witchcraft was something different. It made me feel special." She paused. "And it still does make me feel special," she continued. "But in a different way. Now I feel special because I know that I'm a strong person, that I can make real changes in my life."

"And you think you learned this because of Wicca?" Dr. Hagen asked.

"I think the challenges I've faced while studying Wicca showed me a lot about myself," Kate answered. "There are things I've been through that I never would have been through if it wasn't for the Craft. I've met people I would never have met. I've asked myself questions I would never have asked. I've definitely seen and done things I never would have seen or done."

"What about Tyler?" the doctor asked. "Your parents were concerned that you stayed involved in Wicca because of him."

Kate laughed. "Well, he certainly made it more appealing, at least at the beginning," she said. "But I think I learned more when I was forced to be away from him than I did when we were together. That made me see what was really important."

She couldn't help but think about Annie, and about what had happened between her and Tyler. Once again she felt the ember in her stomach flare up, but this time its heat was much less than it had been before. "I learned that there are more important things than boyfriends," she said suddenly. "There are friendships, and there's myself." She looked at the doctor. "That's the most important thing I've learned," she said, coming to a realization. "I've learned that finding out who I am, and what I can do with my life, is more important than anything else."

She sat back in her chair happily. Instead of feeling like she was being tested and not coming up with the answers, she felt as if she'd just passed with flying colors. Dr. Hagen put her pad down and nodded.

"When you first came in here, you were very angry," she said. "I remember thinking that maybe your parents were right."

"And what do you think now?" Kate asked, turning the tables on her questioner.

"I think you're a remarkable young woman," said Dr. Hagen. "I think you've learned a great deal about yourself."

"Thanks to Wicca," Kate said.

"Perhaps," said the doctor vaguely.

"You don't think studying Wicca has been good for me?" asked Kate, surprised by the doctor's response.

"I think you've learned a lot about yourself," the therapist repeated. "And yes, I think being involved in Wicca has been part of that. Would you have done it otherwise? Who knows?"

"But you think I should keep studying, right?" asked Kate, concerned. Suddenly she was afraid that Dr. Hagen might be siding with her parents.

"I think you should keep questioning and

looking," the doctor replied. "That's always a good thing. Maybe you'll decide to remain in Wicca, maybe you won't. That's not for me to tell you."

"But you're not going to tell my parents I shouldn't stay in class," said Kate, wanting confirmation.

Dr. Hagen shook her head. "No," she said. "I'm going to tell them that I think you're a thoughtful, levelheaded person who can make her own decisions about such things."

Kate sighed. "Thank Goddess," she said. "You had me worried for a minute there."

"Just don't prove me wrong," Dr. Hagen said. "They'll want a refund."

The two of them laughed. Then Dr. Hagen clapped her hands together. "Well, I'm going to have a few words with your parents," she said. "Other than that, I think we're done."

"Really?" Kate said. "You mean I don't have to come back?"

"Not unless you want to," said the therapist. "Do you?"

It was a question she'd asked Kate before. The last time she'd posed it, Kate had said that yes, she wanted to keep coming back. She'd had things to talk about. When she thought about it now, though, she found that she had run out of things to say.

"No," she told the doctor. "I don't want to come

back. Not that I don't like you or anything," she added quickly.

"Don't worry," said Dr. Hagen. "I'm not offended."

The two of them stood up. "It's been fun," Kate said.

"I'm glad you enjoyed yourself," said the therapist. "You've been good company yourself."

"I'm glad Father Mahoney recommended you," Kate said, thinking about the priest at her family's church and how he had suggested the Morgans bring Kate to Dr. Hagen.

"So am I," the doctor replied.

Kate wasn't sure what to do next. She sort of wanted to hug the doctor, but that seemed weird. So instead she walked to the door. "I'll tell my parents to come in," she said. "And thanks again."

She gave the doctor a final wave and left the office. She walked into the waiting room. "She wants to talk to you guys," she told her parents, who were sitting in their usual seats.

Her mother and father made their way down the hall while Kate sat and thumbed through a magazine. She remembered the first time she'd walked into the office, and how mad and scared and apprehensive she'd been. She'd hated her parents for making her see a shrink, and she'd hated the shrink for being what she perceived as an enemy. But everything had changed since that Saturday in September when she'd first met Dr. Hagen. Now she sat in the same office, in the same chair, as she had that first time, but she was a different person.

A few minutes later her parents returned. She looked at their faces, trying to gauge their reactions to whatever Dr. Hagen had said to them. Her mother seemed relaxed and happy, while her father's face wore a slightly strained expression. He didn't seem angry or upset, just a little defeated.

"Well?" Kate asked, her curiosity getting the better of her.

"We can go," her father said simply.

That was good enough for Kate. She stood up, zipped her coat closed, and walked with her parents out to the car. As her father went around to unlock the driver's side door, her mother leaned over and whispered in her ear, "He's just mad because you turned out to be right."

Kate giggled and got into the car. As far as she was concerned, she'd just received the best birthday present ever. But she knew that there was still more to come. There was the party with Annie and Cooper and Sasha that night. They were all having dinner at Annie's house, she knew that much. Then, maybe, they would go to a movie or just hang out. Nothing too exciting. She was just looking forward to being with her best friends.

When she got home she spent a couple of hours helping her mother prepare for the event she was catering that night. It was an anniversary party, and the menu was pretty standard, so they could do it quickly. Luckily, Mrs. Morgan had hired a few part-time people to help her out since beginning her catering business, so Kate no longer had to go with her to help serve. That gave her time to prepare for her own party without hurrying.

She arrived at Annie's house at a little before five. She was surprised to see Cooper's car already there. *She's never on time*, Kate thought as she walked to the front door.

She was even more surprised when Meg answered the door. "Hi," she said. "Come on in."

Kate walked into the Crandalls' house. As she took her coat off she looked around. "Where is everyone?" she asked Meg.

"Out," Meg said simply, taking Kate's coat and hanging it on one of the hooks in the hallway. "Come on."

Bewildered, Kate followed Meg as she walked toward the living room. What did she mean, everyone was out? Why was Cooper's car parked outside if she wasn't here? It didn't make any sense.

Meg disappeared into the living room. As Kate followed her the lights in the room suddenly came on and Kate was greeted with a cry of "Surprise!"

Momentarily shocked, she stood there, blinking and not knowing what was happening. When she finally regained her senses she realized that there were people staring at her—a lot of people.

"What?" she said helplessly, looking around.

She saw Cooper, and Annie, and Sasha, but she also saw Archer, Sophia, Thatcher, Thea, and a lot of other people she knew, including her friends Tara and Jessica. Kate could only stare at them. Then she looked at Annie. "I thought it was just going to be the four of us," she said.

Annie grinned. "That's what we wanted you to think," she said. "Come on. There's more."

She took Kate by the hand and led her into the kitchen. When they got there, Kate couldn't believe her eyes. Her mother was standing at the sink, rinsing strawberries.

"Hi, honey," she said.

"But—" Kate said, taken aback. When she finally realized what was going on she said, "You made me help you prepare my own birthday party?"

Her mother laughed. "Look on the bright side," she said. "Now you get to taste that white chocolate raspberry cake you were drooling over this afternoon."

Kate was overwhelmed with happiness. She couldn't believe that her friends and her mother had gone to so much trouble for her. She turned and hugged Annie, Cooper, and Sasha.

"Thanks, guys," she said.

"And you haven't even seen the presents yet," Sasha said.

They went back to the living room. Someone had turned on music, and everyone was talking and laughing. Soon Mrs. Morgan's helpers came out with trays of food, and before long people were stuffing themselves with her goodies. Everyone came around to wish Kate a happy birthday, and she greeted each one with a hug and a kiss.

"Your mother knows how to cook," said Kate's friend Madelaine, taking a bite of a miniature spinach-and-cheese quiche. "Don't let my mother have this recipe or I'll weigh three hundred pounds next time you see me."

"How did you get all of these people here?" Kate asked Annie as she looked around the room. It was odd seeing people from different parts of her life in the same room. Even Kyle was there, talking to one of the men from the Coven of the Green Wood.

"It took a lot of telephone calls," Annie said. "But I think I got just about everybody."

"Cooper, someone is here to see you," Meg said.

The girls turned around and saw Jane standing there. Cooper went over and gave her a hug, then took Jane by the hand and dragged her over to the others.

"You know everybody, I think," she said.

"Hi," said Jane, sounding nervous.

"*Now* everybody is here," said Kate. "I'm glad you came."

Jane brightened. Then Sasha took her by the arm, pulling her away from Cooper. "Okay," she said. "She's mine now. Come on, I'll introduce you to some cool people."

Sasha and Jane disappeared. Cooper sighed. "I'm so glad she came," she said. "She needed to get out."

"You sound a little stressed," Kate said. "Is everything all right?"

"I'm worried about my mother," Cooper said. "She's having a tough time. But I'll tell you guys about it later. Right now it's time to party."

For the next hour Kate lost herself in the excitement of the party, laughing with her friends and introducing people who didn't yet know one another. When Annie announced that it was time to open presents, she'd almost forgotten that the party was all about *her*. But when she saw the table piled with gifts, she was secretly glad that it was.

"This one is from me," Annie said, handing Kate a large package wrapped in brown paper. "Sorry about the boring paper. I just got it back this afternoon."

Intrigued, Kate tore the paper off and revealed the painting underneath. It was the one Annie had completed during her ritual a few days before. She'd had it framed. Kate looked at the image for a minute.

"It reminds me of a fire," she said. "Like a ritual fire."

Annie beamed. "Do you like it?" she asked.

"I love it," said Kate. "It's so witchy."

Annie put the painting to the side and handed Kate another present. One by one, Kate opened her gifts, oohing and aahing over each one. She was amazed at the things her friends had gotten for her. From Cooper she received a beautiful silver ring in a Celtic knotwork design, and Sasha gave her a pretty scarf made out of incredibly soft wool the color of blueberries. Soon a pile of presents sat at her feet, including incense and candles from the women at Crones' Circle, CDs from Tara and Jessica, a small Goddess statue that Thatcher had carved for her, and, most surprising, a book about Goddess stories from around the world from Kyle.

"We helped him pick it out," Annie whispered to Kate as she looked from her brother to the book and back again.

Almost as soon as Kate unwrapped her last gift, her mother appeared carrying a cake covered in candles. The room burst into the traditional birthday song, and Kate obliged everyone by blowing out the sixteen candles. Then plates were handed around and she found herself eating the most wonderful cake she'd ever had. She had two more pieces before declaring herself totally stuffed.

As the party wound down, people left in groups of two and three, and before long it was just Annie, Kate, Cooper, Sasha, Jane, and a few others who stayed around to help clean up. The girls sat in the living room talking while they recovered from the excitement of the past few hours.

"Those women from Crones' Circle were really cool," Jane said. "I'm glad I got to talk to them."

"So, are you going to take the class when it

starts up again in April?" Sasha asked her. "We can be witches-in-training together if you do."

Jane gave her a coy look. "You never know," she said.

"Madelaine was talking about that, too," said Annie thoughtfully. "Interesting."

"Kate, your mother's food was out of this world," said Cooper.

"Hey," Kate said. "Don't forget, I made some of that, too."

"Your brother wasn't half bad, either," remarked Sasha. "He's a hottie."

Kate made a face. "Please," she said. "*Kyle* and *hottie* are two words I don't think I can face in the same sentence."

"Kate?"

Kate turned. Meg was standing in the doorway. "There's someone here to see you," she said.

"I'll be right back," Kate said, getting up.

She walked to the front door. When she saw Tyler standing there, she froze. He smiled slightly.

"Hey," he said.

"Hey there," Kate replied. *What are you doing here?* She wanted to add, but didn't.

"I know I shouldn't have come," he said. "But I heard there was a party, and I wanted to give you something." He held out his hand. In it was a wrapped box.

Kate walked over to him. She reached out and hesitantly took the gift. "You didn't have to," she said.

"I know I didn't have to," said Tyler. "I wanted to."

Kate unwrapped the gift. Inside was a picture. It was of her and Tyler. They were sitting on a beach, and Tyler had his arm around her. They were both smiling.

"Willow took it at Beltane," Tyler said. "I found it a few days ago and it made me happy to look at it. I thought maybe it would make you happy, too."

Kate looked at the picture. She didn't know how it made her feel.

"I hope we can be friends again, Kate," Tyler said. "I'd like that."

Kate shut her eyes tightly, then opened them again. She was finding it hard to speak. She looked up and directly into Tyler's eyes. *They're golden*, she thought randomly. She was trying to think of something to say, but nothing was coming.

Before she could speak, Tyler leaned forward and kissed her gently on the cheek. "Happy birthday," he said. Then he turned and walked out of the house, leaving her standing there looking at the picture in her hands and unable to think about anything else except the lingering feeling of his lips on her skin.

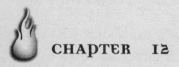

CHAPTER 12

"I've got Annie's chart here," Olivia Sorensen announced at the start of class on Tuesday night. "And an interesting chart it is."

She waved a piece of paper in the air. It was covered with charts and boxes filled with strange symbols, and Annie wondered what they all meant. She was still doubtful about the whole thing, but she had to admit she was also curious to hear what Olivia had to say about her.

"As I told you last week, I always ask a few questions to make sure that I've done the chart correctly. So I'd like to start with those if that's okay."

"It's fine with me," said Annie.

Olivia looked at the chart. "Okay," she said. "Can you tell me about the time when you were about four years old and something dramatic happened to you involving water."

Annie nodded. "I almost drowned when I was four," she said, surprised. "At the beach."

"I thought so," said Olivia. "Okay, how about when you were six?" she continued. "Something else big happened, but this time involving fire."

Annie froze up. The fire. She'd been six. Again, she found it hard to believe that the astrologer could see that. But she did. Did she also see that Annie's parents had died in that fire? If she did, she wasn't saying anything. Annie simply said, "Yes, that's right." She could see Kate and Cooper looking at her, checking to make sure she was okay. She looked at her friends and tried to appear calm.

"Great," Olivia said. "This is looking good, but let's keep going. "When you were twelve, did you travel somewhere, and I mean somewhere sort of exotic, not just like to another state or anything?"

"We went to Cancún," Annie answered. "For a vacation."

"That explains the sun," Olivia said distractedly, making a note on the paper. "One final question. How old were you when you started studying the Craft?"

"Fifteen," Annie answered.

"Perfect," Olivia said. "The chart matches up just right."

"How did you see all of those things?" asked Cooper. "You were pretty specific."

Olivia nodded. "I can be very specific," she said. "Different planets, and the combinations of planets with each other, suggest certain types of events. For example, when I asked Annie about the incident with water, it was because at that point in her life there was a very strong Neptune influence. Neptune, of course, was the god of water, and the planet Neptune often suggests the influence of water. She also had a very strong Pluto influence at that time. Pluto, the god of the underworld, was connected with death, as is the planet named after him. Those two things combined suggested to me that perhaps Annie had had some dangerous encounter with water. And, as it turned out, she had."

"Why did you ask me about when I started studying the Craft?" Annie inquired.

"Two Decembers ago, there was an interesting combination of planets in your chart," Olivia explained. "One was Jupiter, a planet that influences things like learning and thinking about serious subjects such as spirituality. Another was Mars. Mars suggests adventure and trying new things. And the third planet was Venus, which suggests feminine principles. These three planets together suggested to me that perhaps you developed an interest in Wicca around that time."

Annie thought for a moment. "It *was* right around then that I started reading more about it," she said. "But I didn't really get involved seriously until February and March," she added, "when I met Kate and Cooper."

"That makes sense," Olivia replied. "The influence began in December and grew stronger throughout the spring. I imagine if we did Kate's and Cooper's charts we'd find that they had similar influences operating during that time."

"Wow," Cooper said. "This is pretty amazing."

"It certainly can be," said Olivia. "Once you start seeing how all these different influences combine to form patterns, it can help you see why certain patterns occur in your life."

"What does Annie's chart say about her?" Kate asked.

Olivia held up the paper in her hand and pointed to one of the charts. It was a circle divided into twelve sections, like a pie. Each one was numbered and had a list of words in it. Some of the sections had symbols around their edges as well, while others had just the words.

"This chart shows the twelve different houses, or sections, of the astrological chart," explained Olivia. "Each house is associated with different personality traits. This one, for example," she said, pointing to the section numbered 9, "has to do with spirituality, travel, and your connection to the larger world."

"What are those symbols around the edge?" asked a woman behind Cooper.

"Those are the planets that were located in that astrological house at the time of Annie's birth," Olivia told her. "This one is Jupiter," she said, pointing to one of the symbols. "As I said earlier, Jupiter is connected to a person's interest in philosophical subjects. So looking at this, I would guess that Annie has always been interested in things like spirituality."

"That's true," Annie said. "But I'm also very scientific. Where does that come in?"

"Right here," answered Olivia, pointing to one of the other houses on the chart. "This is the house of learning, particularly learning of an organized, logical kind. In that house you have the planet Mercury. That indicates a way of thinking that is more analytical and less abstract. I bet you're good at math, too, right?"

"She's a year ahead of the rest of us," Cooper said.

"There are other interesting things in your chart," said Olivia. "Without getting into too much detail, I'd say that you tend to be very realistic and not prone to fantasy. I'd also venture a guess that you're not very likely to take a lot of risks, but when you do you really go for it."

Annie listened to Olivia's assessment of her personality. It was a little frightening how accurate it was.

"You tend to be a bit of a loner," said Olivia, scanning the chart. "Mainly because you don't feel like you fit in a lot of the time. And you have very strong ties to your family, particularly your siblings. Does that all sound right?"

"Almost perfect," Annie said. "Except the part about my siblings. I only have one."

Olivia wrinkled her brow. "That's funny," she

said. "The chart really suggests that you have at least two." She paused for a moment. "Well, that might just be me reading it. As I said before, this isn't an exact science. The important thing is that we have a basic blueprint of your astrological profile."

"Can you tell things about Annie's future from that chart as well?" asked Kate.

"Sure," Olivia replied. "At least I can look at the basic influences and what they might indicate. That's what I do when I do readings for people. But I'm not going to do that right now. This was just a demonstration to explain a little bit about how an astrological birth chart works. What we're going to do tonight is talk about the different planets and what parts of our personalities and lives they're said to affect."

Annie listened for the next half an hour as Olivia went through the planets and their associations, but she wasn't really listening. Instead, she was thinking about what the astrologer had said about her. It unnerved her that so much of her personality and her life could be revealed by looking at her astrological chart. She'd always prided herself on being a unique individual, and now she felt a little like some kind of puppet being controlled by a bunch of planets and stars. Did they really have that much to say about how she lived? The idea was disturbing.

At the end of class she rode home on the bus with her friends, as usual. Kate and Cooper couldn't stop talking about how exciting class had been, and about how they would love to have their charts done by Olivia.

"Imagine, finding out what might happen to you," said Kate. "That would be cool."

"Unless you had some really bad planets coming along," Cooper mused. "But I'd even like to know about that."

"What did you think of her reading, Annie?" Kate asked.

Annie, who had been staring aimlessly out the window at the passing cars, turned and shrugged. "I don't know," she said. "It was interesting, but I'm still not sure I believe it."

"Come on," Cooper said. "Look at all of those things she knew about you."

Annie nodded. "I know," she said. "But even Olivia admitted that a lot of it was guesswork. She saw a planet connected with water and one with death and she put them together. She could just as easily have guessed that I overwatered a rosebush and it croaked."

Cooper gave her a look that clearly indicated she thought Annie was being ridiculous. Annie refused to give in, saying, "I'm serious. Do you really think that because I was born at a certain time and in a certain place I'm going to be more interested in spirituality or politics or art than anyone else?"

"It's as good a reason as any," Cooper answered.

"I don't think it is," argued Annie. "I mean,

look, my parents were the same way. Probably I got it from them. And if all this is true, does that mean that every baby born in the same hospital I was, and at the same time as I was, has the same life I do? Think about it."

Her friends sat quietly, not saying anything for a minute. Annie, however, was taking her own advice and thinking about what she'd just said. And she wasn't happy with what she was coming up with. The truth was, it bothered her that the astrology stuff made so much sense. It bothered her a lot. She knew that she was being argumentative because she really did want her friends to prove her wrong, or at least agree with her that it was all a lot of lucky guessing on Olivia's part. But they weren't cooperating.

"I still think it's cool," Cooper said as they neared their stop, earning herself a vicious glare from Annie. "Well, it *is*," she said again.

They got off and said their good-byes to one another. As Annie walked home, she tried not to think about astrology. But she couldn't help it. Finally she stopped and looked up at the sky. Above her the stars twinkled brightly. She'd always thought of stars as being cheerful, happy things. Now, though, she imagined them, millions of miles away, having a secret meeting to decide her fate.

"I know," she imagined one of them saying to the others, "let's get Pluto over here and send Annie a really bad day. Maybe we'll have her kiss her best friend's boyfriend."

"Good idea," she pictured another one chiming in. "*And* we'll give her frizzy hair."

"And a zit," added a third.

"Thanks a lot, you guys," she said to the sky, and continued walking.

When she reached her house she went inside and hung her coat up. She saw her aunt sitting in the living room, and she went in to see what she was doing. Aunt Sarah was curled up on the couch, reading a book.

"Hi," she said when she saw Annie come in. "How was class?"

"Weird," Annie replied, flopping down in an armchair.

"Weird how?" asked Aunt Sarah.

"We're talking about astrology," Annie explained. "Tonight the woman running the class did my chart. It was just weird."

"Did she say you were going to meet a tall, dark, handsome stranger?" Aunt Sarah teased.

"I wish," said Annie. "No, she didn't say anything like that. In fact, she said really nice stuff. It just bothered me that she could do that. It was like someone had done a background check on me or something. There she was, looking at some stars and planets and telling me that I'm good at science and that I almost drowned when I was little."

Her aunt whistled. "That is a little weird," she said.

"She knew about the fire," Annie continued.

"And she knew about our trip to Mexico. Not the details, but she might as well have."

"That would freak me out, too," said Aunt Sarah.

Annie sighed. "At least she had one strike," she said. "She said that the chart showed I had two siblings."

"What?" Aunt Sarah asked.

"Two siblings," Annie repeated. "But it's just me and Meg, so she was wrong about that. For a minute, though, I thought maybe I was the one who was wrong about it. She'd been right about everything else."

"She said the chart showed you had two siblings?" her aunt asked.

"Yeah," said Annie. "But she said she might just have misread it, too."

Her aunt didn't say anything. She just nodded, then seemed to look at something on the wall. Annie watched her for a moment. There was something odd about the expression on her aunt's face, something that troubled her.

"What?" Annie said. "Is there, like, a giant spider up there about to fall on my head. If there is, just nod and I'll die right now."

Her aunt shook her head. "No," she said. "It isn't that."

"Then what?" Annie asked again. "You look like you just got really terrible news."

Aunt Sarah smiled sadly. "I was just thinking

about something," she said. She looked at Annie for a long moment. "Maybe it's time you knew."

"Knew what?" said Annie. The way her aunt was looking at her was making her nervous. Then she had a sudden thought. "You're not pregnant, are you?" she asked, her eyes widening.

It was Aunt Sarah's turn to say "What?" Then she laughed. "No, I'm not pregnant." She looked thoughtful for a moment, as if she was considering the possibility seriously. "No," she said again. "Definitely not."

"Then I'm a little lost here," Annie said. "What's the big news?"

Aunt Sarah sat on the edge of the couch. "Do you know how your parents met?" she asked.

"Not really," Annie said. "In college, I think."

Aunt Sarah nodded. "That's right," she said. "Well, sort of. They were both *in* college, but not the same one. Your mother and I were friends, and one time she came home with me over a long weekend. That's when she met my brother—and your father."

"I didn't know that," Annie said, delighted by the news. "That's so cool. And they fell in love and got married. How perfect."

"Well, not so perfect," Aunt Sarah said. "They didn't exactly like each other at first. In fact, their first meeting involved your mother telling your father that he was wearing the ugliest shirt she'd ever seen."

Annie laughed. "I can imagine that," she said,

thinking about all the times her mother had teased her father about his choice of clothes.

"But they liked each other enough that she agreed to go out with him when she came for the next long weekend," Aunt Sarah continued. "And then they realized that they had a lot more in common than they'd thought."

Annie was enjoying hearing about this part of her parents' relationship. She'd been too young when they died to really know anything about it, and she'd never asked her aunt. Now that the story was coming out, she was anxious to hear more.

"The two of them were more in love than any couple I've ever known," Aunt Sarah said. "When they were apart they called each other every day, and when they were together they were inseparable."

She stopped talking and the faraway look returned to her eyes. Annie waited for her to continue, wondering where the story was going.

"The summer before our senior year, your mother stayed with our family for a few weeks before we went back to school," Aunt Sarah said. "Then one night about a month after we returned to school, she came to my room. She was upset."

"Why?" Annie asked. "Had she and my father had a fight or something?"

"No," Aunt Sarah said, smiling faintly. "She was pregnant."

Annie's mouth dropped open. "Pregnant?" she

said. *"My* mother?"

Aunt Sarah nodded. "Your mother," she said.

"What?" Annie said. "How?" She had all kinds of questions, but she couldn't get any of them out. Her mother had been pregnant? How could she not have known that?

"What did you do?" she asked finally.

"We talked about her options," said Aunt Sarah. "We went over the choices she had, and what the pros and cons of each of them were. We talked all night. And by the morning she'd made her decision."

"She had an abortion?" asked Annie quietly.

Aunt Sarah shook her head. "She had the baby," she said.

Once again Annie's mouth dropped open. "She had it?" she said.

"Yes," said Aunt Sarah. "She and your father talked about it, and she decided to have it." She laughed. "It seems strange now, but you wouldn't believe what we went through to keep the fact that she was pregnant a secret from your grandparents."

"Why did it have to be a secret?" asked Annie.

"Oh," Aunt Sarah said, "your mother's father was *very* strict. He would have totally flipped out if he'd known."

"How could you hide something like that?" Annie asked.

"It wasn't easy, believe me," said Aunt Sarah. "Luckily, her family lived far away. The only time your mother had to go home was at Christmas, and she wasn't very big yet. She had the baby in May, and your grandparents never knew. Only our family did, and we all agreed never to talk about it."

Annie was dumbfounded. She couldn't even begin to take in everything she was hearing. Her mother had had another baby. "What happened to it?" she asked.

"She gave it up for adoption," said Aunt Sarah. "She and Peter knew that they weren't ready to be parents yet. They were just starting out. So she agreed to let someone adopt it who could take care of it and give it a loving home."

Aunt Sarah was looking at Annie closely. "I know this is hard to hear," she said. "I'd sort of decided never to tell you girls about it. But for some reason I think you should know."

Annie nodded. "I'm glad you told me," she said. Then another question came to her. "What was it?" she asked. "The baby, I mean. Was it a boy or a girl?"

"A girl," Aunt Sarah said. "And Annie, anything you want to know about this, just ask."

Annie nodded. She heard her aunt, but she wasn't really listening. She was too busy thinking about what the news meant. *A sister*, she thought. *I have another sister somewhere.*

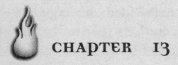 **CHAPTER 13**

Cooper picked at the piece of bread in her hand, taking tiny pieces and popping them into her mouth. She didn't even taste it as she chewed, but the repetitive motion of grinding it between her teeth made her feel better. It gave her something to concentrate on while she figured out how to say what she needed to say.

"How's your dinner?"

Cooper looked up. Across the table, her father was looking at her with a concerned expression. He had already eaten half of the chicken marsala he'd ordered, and he was busily cutting up the remaining portion. He looked meaningfully at Cooper's sea bass, which remained mostly untouched.

"Oh, it's great," said Cooper, attempting to sound enthusiastic. She picked up her fork and jabbed the sea bass with it, taking a big bite. "Mmm," she said as she swallowed it.

"Okay," said her father. "You're not fooling me. What's going on?"

Cooper put down the fork. She took a sip of water from her glass. Finally, there was nothing else she could do to distract herself.

"It's Mom," she said, knowing that now that she'd begun the conversation she was going to have to see it through.

"Your mother?" her father said. "What about her?"

Cooper sat back in her chair. She and her father were at La Mer, one of the city's nicest restaurants. Normally, Cooper loved the place, with its chic but comfortable decor and the blue lights that made it look as if patrons were dining under water. But tonight they might as well have been at Burger King.

"She's really depressed," Cooper said.

Her father nodded. "That's to be expected," he said. "A divorce is really difficult on everyone, even when you know it's the right thing."

"It's more than that," said Cooper. She paused, not sure if she should tell him the rest. "She's been drinking."

Her father looked up, concern in his eyes. "Drinking?" he said. "Your mother doesn't drink. I mean, she'll have wine with dinner, or maybe a cocktail every so often, but she doesn't drink very much."

"She does now," Cooper informed him. She told him about finding her mother practically passed out on the sofa on Friday night. She also told him about the conversation she'd tried to have with her when she got back from Jane's, a conversation that had not gone well at all.

"What did she say?" he asked.

"She told me she was fine," replied Cooper. "She said she'd just had a few drinks to unwind after a long day." She shook her head. "But it was more than that, Dad," she said. "She's been acting weird for a while now. This is just the latest thing. I'm really worried."

Her father didn't say anything for a minute. He pushed his food around his plate, not eating it. At one point he reached for the glass of wine beside his water glass, but then he pulled his hand away, not touching it.

"What would you like me to do?" he asked his daughter.

"I don't know," said Cooper. "I don't know what you *can* do. I don't know what *I* can do. I feel really weird talking to her. I mean, she's my mother. She's the one who's supposed to worry about me."

Mr. Rivers smiled to himself. "I think that's the first time I've ever heard you admit that *you're* the child in that relationship," he said.

"You know Mom and I don't see things the same way," said Cooper. "That doesn't mean I don't love her, or that I don't worry about her. But this isn't something I can do for her."

"Do you want me to talk to her?" asked her father.

Cooper sighed. "Then she'd know I told you,"

she said. "She'd freak."

"What if we make it look like I found out by accident?" Mr. Rivers suggested.

Cooper looked at him, shocked. "You mean trick her?" she asked. "How?"

"How about after dinner I drive you home," he said. "I can come in with you. We'll say that there's something I left at the house that I need to pick up. There's no reason I shouldn't do that."

Cooper thought about his proposal. "That would work," she said.

"How was your mother when you left to come here?" asked her father.

"She'd had a drink or two," said Cooper. "I think she was settling in for the night."

"Good," Mr. Rivers said. "I mean, it's not *good*, but it might work for what we want to do. If I can catch your mother in the act, so to speak, I can legitimately talk to her about this."

"Man, you really *are* a lawyer, aren't you?" Cooper said.

"You say that like it's a bad thing," her father teased.

"In this case I guess it isn't," said Cooper. "I just hate that we have to do it at all."

Mr. Rivers took another bite of chicken. "Your mother is in pain," he said, sounding sad. "When people hurt they do a lot of things to try and feel better. Your mother is just trying to stop hurting. I understand that."

"Then why aren't you doing the same thing?" asked Cooper.

Her father fixed her with a look. "You ask a lot of questions," he said. "Are you sure you aren't going to be the next lawyer in the family?"

Cooper snorted. "Right," she said. "I'm going to be lucky to graduate from high school with my grades."

"Speaking of which . . ." her father said.

Cooper narrowed her eyes. "I don't think I like the sound of that," she said.

Her father looked at her. "It's probably time we started talking about college," he said.

Cooper groaned. She'd been trying to forget about the college issue ever since T.J. had brought it up during their walk. She'd sort of been hoping that in all of the tumult surrounding her parents' divorce they would just forget about it somehow. *I should have known better*, she thought grimly.

"You have to go to college," said her father.

"Why?" Cooper said petulantly, although inside she knew he was right.

"Have you given it any thought?" asked Mr. Rivers, ignoring her rhetorical question.

"I haven't even finished junior year," responded Cooper. "How am I supposed to know what I want to do more than a year from now?"

Her father put down his fork and wiped his mouth. "You can't tell me you haven't even *thought* about what you might want to study," he said. "I don't buy that for a minute."

Cooper remained silent. The truth was, she *had* thought about what she wanted to study, and the problem was that she hadn't really come up with any concrete ideas. She was interested in a lot of things—music, writing, and art, to name a few. But she also found things like religion and philosophy interesting, particularly since she'd begun studying Wicca. She thought she might like to study those things, but she didn't know what she would ever do with a degree in something like philosophy. And while she loved playing music, she wasn't sure it was something she could ever make a living at.

"No one is asking you to decide the rest of your life right this second," her father told her. "But it *is* important to pick a school that will help you get where you want to go."

Cooper knew what he was getting at. Mr. Rivers had gone to a famous Ivy League school. She knew that one of the reasons behind his success was that he was still friends with a lot of the people he'd gone to school with. He had often told her that getting ahead was 75 percent hard work and 25 percent networking.

"I don't want to be in any kind of business where the school I went to matters," she said carefully. She respected her father and what he did, even if she often teased him about it, and she didn't want to make him feel bad. "I want to go to a school where I feel like I'm free to explore," she said.

She saw a smile flicker across her father's face, but it disappeared before it turned into a smirk. She knew he thought she was being idealistic. But she was really just being honest. Something else she'd learned from her study of witchcraft was that being open to lots of possibilities was important for finding out who she really was and what she could do with her talents.

"I'm serious," she said.

"I know you are," replied her father. "I'm not saying you're not. It's just that you sound a lot like I did when I was trying to decide where to go to school."

"You?" Cooper said. "I thought you always wanted to be a lawyer."

Her father shook his head. "I wanted to be an archaeologist," he said, laughing.

Cooper gave him a look indicating she thought he was pulling her leg. Her father, the lawyer, an archaeologist? The idea was too funny to take seriously.

"I did," he said, noting her expression. "I loved reading about adventurers when I was younger. I thought it would be wonderful to go to places I'd never been and see what I could find there."

"But . . ." Cooper said, wondering how his life had taken such a dramatic turn.

"But my father wanted me to do something practical," said Mr. Rivers. "So I studied history in college to satisfy myself and then went on to law school."

"Sounds like a compromise to me," Cooper said.

"I guess it was," said her father. "But I like law, so no regrets."

"None?" asked Cooper doubtfully.

"Well, maybe a few little ones," her father said. "The point is, I want you to do whatever it is you dream of doing, but I also want you to be a little bit practical."

"Fair enough," said Cooper. "I'll start thinking about schools." She hesitated before adding, "What do you think of Rummond?"

"Rummond?" her father said. "The school in Minnesota?"

"Uh-huh," said Cooper, trying to sound nonchalant.

"I guess it's an okay school," said Mr. Rivers. "But there's nothing special about it. Why?"

"Just asking," Cooper said. "I have a friend who might be going there."

Her father nodded. "This friend," he said, "his name wouldn't be T.J., would it?"

"Wow," Cooper said, suddenly engrossed in the dessert menu. "Did you see they have flan?"

"Cooper . . ." Mr. Rivers said.

Cooper put down the menu and looked at her father. He was looking back at her warmly. "Don't tell me my daughter is actually considering going to a school to follow some boy."

Cooper rolled her eyes. "I was just *asking*," she

said. "You don't need to put me on the witness stand."

Her father laughed. Then he folded his hands. "I know this is a hard time for you," he said. "You're dealing with your mother and me. You have to think about college and your future. There are a lot of choices to make. Just promise me that when you make them the only person you'll take into consideration is you."

"Don't worry," said Cooper. "I promise to be totally self-centered and egotistical when the time comes."

"That's my girl," said her father.

The waiter brought the check, Cooper's father paid, and they left the restaurant. Only instead of walking home, Cooper got into her father's car and they drove back to the house on Welton Street. When they pulled up outside it, her father turned the engine off and looked at the windows. The living room was lit up.

"I'm assuming your mother is in there," he said. He sounded sad. "It's strange looking at that house and knowing it isn't home anymore."

"What's the plan?" Cooper asked him.

"We'll go in," said Mr. Rivers. "I'll tell your mother that I need to get something from the attic. That will make sense. There's so much stuff up there it's entirely believable that I would leave something behind. And then we'll take it from there."

"Sounds good," said Cooper. "Ready?"

"Lead the way," said her father.

They got out of the car and walked to the door. Cooper used her key to open it, and they stepped inside.

"Mom?" Cooper called out, not wanting to take her mother by surprise. A big part of her hoped that her mother would call out in her normal voice and that she would find out that the drinking incident had been a onetime thing she'd blown way out of proportion.

But there was no response. Still, there was music coming from the living room. Cooper and her father walked in there. Mrs. Rivers was on the couch, a glass in her hand. Her head was thrown back against the pillows and she was humming.

"Hi," Cooper said again.

Mrs. Rivers opened her eyes and looked at her daughter. She smiled slowly. "I didn't hear you come in," she said.

"Hello, Janet," said Mr. Rivers.

Mrs. Rivers looked at her husband, an expression of confusion on her face.

"What are you doing here?" she asked, sounding both irritated and surprised.

"Dad needs to get something out of the attic," said Cooper, sticking with the game plan they'd established.

"Fine," said her mother, closing her eyes and beginning to hum again.

Mr. Rivers went over and turned off the music. Cooper's mother turned her head and glared at him.

"Why'd you do that?" she asked.

Mr. Rivers looked at Cooper. "I think we all need to talk," he said.

Mrs. Rivers laughed. "Talk?" she said, suddenly sounding a lot more sober than Cooper thought she was. "Didn't we already do all of our talking, Stephen?"

"I don't mean about us," Mr. Rivers replied. "I mean about you, and about what you're doing."

Mrs. Rivers sat up. She looked at Cooper, then at her husband. "And what exactly am I doing?" she asked.

There was an icy silence. Cooper felt as if the room were closing in on her. It seemed too small, and she couldn't breathe. She wanted some air. She wanted to run back outside and get away from the feelings of frustration she felt rising in her. But she tried to calm herself so that she could say what she needed to say.

"I'm worried about you, Mom," Cooper said. "It's like I said to you the other night, I think maybe you're—"

She didn't know how to finish the sentence. All of the possible endings sounded like accusations, and she didn't want to make her mother feel cornered. She knew how that felt, and it wasn't a good feeling. She wanted her mother to feel loved and cared for. But she didn't know how to do that.

"Think maybe I'm what?" said her mother. "Drinking too much? Is that it?"

"Maybe," Cooper said, looking at her.

"I'm fine," said Mrs. Rivers. "Don't worry about it." Then she looked at her husband. "Thanks for coming over," she said. "But I think everything is under control. Do you still need to go to the attic?"

"No," Cooper's father said. "I don't think that will be necessary."

"Then I'm going to go to bed," said Mrs. Rivers. "I have to teach in the morning."

She stood up, unsteadily, and walked out of the room. Cooper and her father listened as she walked heavily up the stairs. Then they heard the slam of her bedroom door.

Cooper looked at her father. "That went well," she said. "Really well."

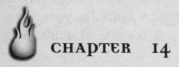

CHAPTER 14

Annie turned the pages of the photo album slowly, looking at each image carefully, as if searching for clues. She was sitting at the kitchen table with her aunt. There was a large cardboard box sitting on one of the empty chairs.

"I haven't looked at these things in years," Aunt Sarah said.

Half an hour before, the two of them had been rummaging around in the basement, peering into musty trunks and boxes and looking at junk that hadn't seen the light of day in a long time. There had been dust everywhere, and spiders, and Annie couldn't wait to find what they were looking for and get back upstairs. Now they were sitting with the treasure they'd gone in search of.

Annie still hadn't quite accepted what her aunt had told her on Tuesday night. When she woke up on Wednesday morning, her first thought was that it had all been a dream. But of course it hadn't been, and that meant that she had to deal with the information she'd been given. For most of the day she'd walked around in a fog, her head filled with images of what her sister might look like.

Her *older* sister, she reminded herself. She'd done the math and figured out that the baby her mother had given up for adoption would be almost seven years older than she was, which would make her twenty-three. It seemed impossible that someone could be walking around who was related to her and she didn't even know it. What had the woman been doing her whole life? What was she like? Did she even know that she had two other sisters? *How could she?* Annie thought. *She probably doesn't even know who her birth mother was.*

For two days Annie had been unable to think of anything else except her older sister. She didn't tell her friends about it because it was too new, too private, and she wasn't sure what there was to even tell them yet. Nor did she say a word to Meg. Her sister was too young to understand. Annie herself didn't even really understand. Besides, her aunt had asked her not to say anything, and Annie had agreed.

But she hadn't agreed to not ask any more questions herself. So that afternoon, after school, she'd asked Aunt Sarah if she could tell her anything else about the baby her mother had given up. Her aunt had looked thoughtful for a moment and then nodded. That was how they'd ended up in the cellar.

Now, in the light-filled kitchen, with cups of peppermint tea in front of them and a plate of brownies nearby ready to be eaten, Annie was hearing more about her mother's life in college.

"No one has seen these pictures besides your parents and I," Aunt Sarah said. "Your mother wanted to have a record of her pregnancy, although she wasn't sure why, so she had me take lots of pictures of her."

Annie nodded. She was staring at a snapshot of her mother sitting on a blanket on some grass. She was smiling and pointing to her belly.

"That was the quad at our college," Aunt Sarah said. "About a month after your mother found out she was pregnant."

"How could she be so happy?" asked Annie. "Wasn't she afraid?"

"She was terrified," her aunt said. "But yes, she was happy. It's hard to explain. It's like she knew the baby was going to have a great life, and that she was the one giving her that life. Once she made the decision to have the baby, it was like she was filled with this strength I'd never seen in her before."

They turned the pages. As they progressed, Annie saw her mother getting bigger and bigger as the baby grew. She also watched the seasons change from late summer to fall to winter. As the weather turned cold, her mother appeared in jackets and scarves. There were pictures of her building a snowman and jumping in a pile of autumn leaves. Annie's father appeared in some of the pictures, always with his arms around her mother and always smiling.

"It must have been hard for them," said Annie. "Knowing that they were going to have to give the baby away, I mean."

Aunt Sarah nodded. "It was hard in a lot of ways," she said. "People at school gave your mother a hard time because she wasn't married and because they never saw her with your dad. And she had to hide her pregnancy from her parents. That was the toughest part."

As they got toward the back of the album, and the end of her mother's pregnancy, the pictures showed a world changing from the frozen whiteness of winter to the newness of spring. Now Annie's mother really looked pregnant, and there were pictures of her sitting at her desk, studying, while she rested her hands on her distended stomach. There was another, which Annie particularly liked, of her mother standing in a field of daffodils beneath a bright spring sun. Her face glowed, and she reminded Annie of an image she'd seen of the Goddess awakening the earth after its long sleep.

"That was right before she gave birth," said Aunt Sarah, touching the picture gently with her finger.

"Were you there for that?" Annie asked.

Her aunt nodded. "So was your father. I remember he had to drive all night to get there in time. She went into labor right after an English Lit exam. I took her to the hospital and called him from there." She laughed. "I'll never forget your mother telling the baby that it had to wait until Peter got there before she would let it come out."

Annie laughed, too. "And it did?"

"Barely," Aunt Sarah said. "Your father got there at dawn and the baby arrived about half an hour later."

Annie turned the last page, and there she saw an image that made her heart stop. It was her mother, sitting in a hospital bed. She was holding a baby in her arms, and she was looking at it. Annie's father stood beside them, also looking at the baby, and both her mother and her father had expressions of joy on their faces.

"I wasn't supposed to take that one," Aunt Sarah said. "The caseworker handling the adoption didn't even want your parents to hold the baby. But they insisted, and while no one was looking I snapped that."

Annie stared at the picture for a long time. First she concentrated on her parents' faces. Then she looked at the baby. It was so small, and it was hard to see anything. But Annie could see its tiny hands waving in the air, and its eyes were open, looking up at her mother and father.

"She saw them," she said softly. "She saw their faces. I bet she doesn't even remember that."

She felt a sharp stab of pain inside of her, looking at the baby in her mother's arms. What must it have been like for her mother, holding her and knowing that she only had a few minutes with her? What had her father thought, looking at his daughter and knowing that someone else was going to take her home? Annie couldn't even imagine. Did they think about changing their minds? Did they wish they'd never had the baby?

"What happened next?" she asked, not really wanting to know the answer but knowing that she had to ask.

"The caseworker came and took the baby," said her aunt slowly. "They didn't want your parents to meet the adoptive parents, so they had them in another room. They thought it would be easier that way."

"So they never saw them?" Annie said.

Her aunt shook her head. "No," she answered. "They didn't. But I did."

Annie looked at her. "I couldn't help it," Aunt Sarah said. "Besides, I'd already taken a picture. I figured I couldn't get into much more trouble. So when she left with the baby I pretended I needed to go to the bathroom and I followed her."

"What were they like?" asked Annie.

"They were a young couple," her aunt replied. "About the same age your parents were when they had you. She had long black hair. I remember that because it was so pretty. He was tall and thin. I saw the caseworker put the baby in her arms. The woman started to cry and her husband hugged her. Then the caseworker saw me looking into the room, so I ran."

That was the end, Annie thought. *That was the last time they saw her.* Her sister had been taken home by strangers while her parents had to go home without her.

She felt her aunt put her arm around her. "I know this all sounds terrible," she said. "But it was really for the best. Your parents went on to finish school and start their lives together. Then, when they were ready, they had you and Meg."

"But didn't they ever wonder?" asked Annie. "Didn't they want to know what happened to her?"

"Sure," her aunt replied. "Who wouldn't? But they knew that her life was meant to go in a different direction from theirs. They'd done what they could for her—they'd given her life."

Once more Annie found herself thinking about fate. Was it really true that this was how things had been meant to be? Had it already been decided that her mother would have a baby and give it up? True, her mother had chosen to have the baby instead of not having it, but was there some larger plan at work that she was just a small part of? And if that was true, was Annie—or Meg, or Aunt Sarah, or all of them—just part of some big game being played out all across the world?

"What are you guys doing?"

Annie looked up and saw Meg coming into the kitchen. She'd been up in her room, reading. Now she approached the photo album with curiosity.

Annie shut the book quickly and put it in her

lap. "It's a project I'm doing for school," Annie said, trying to think of a story to tell her younger sister.

"Can I see it?" asked Meg.

"Not yet," said Annie. "It's not done."

Meg regarded her sister with suspicion. Annie knew that she didn't buy the story, and she half expected Meg to put up a fight. She could be really stubborn when she wanted to be, particularly when she thought something was being kept from her. She and Meg looked at one another, each seemingly waiting for the other to blink.

Finally, Meg took a brownie from the plate and bit into it. "Okay," she said, and Annie breathed a sigh of relief. She looked at her aunt. "I'm going to take this upstairs and work on it."

Her aunt looked at her for a long moment, then nodded, "Good idea," she said. "Why don't you take this stuff with you?" she added, indicating the cardboard box.

Annie put the album into the box and carried the whole thing up the stairs to her room. She set it on her bed and took out the album again. Then she looked at the other things in the box. Mostly they were just more photographs, this time of her aunt and people that Annie didn't know. She sifted through them, enjoying seeing what Aunt Sarah had looked like when she was younger.

Then, underneath the photos, she found something else. It looked like a book, but there was no title on it. Annie picked it up and opened it. Inside she saw that the pages were covered in handwriting. It was a journal. *It must be Aunt Sarah's,* she thought, *from when she was in college.*

She opened the book to the first page. It was dated September 17, 1977.

It's definite—I'm pregnant. I guess I knew I was, but now I know for sure. I still can't really believe it. Me, a mother. I can't even keep the plant in our dorm room alive. How am I supposed to have a baby?

Annie looked at the page in astonishment. It wasn't her aunt's diary, it was her mother's. The handwriting on the pages was hers. Annie reached out and ran her fingers over it, feeling the ink beneath her fingertips. Her mother had written these words on the day she found out she was pregnant. For a moment Annie thought she should shut the diary and put it back. After all, these were her mother's personal thoughts. They were private.

But maybe this is here for a reason, Annie thought. *Maybe I'm supposed to see this.* She continued to read.

I don't know what Peter is going to think. I know he loves me, and I know I love him. But I don't think either of us is ready for a baby. There are so many things we want to do, and we can't take care of a baby right now. I know I don't have to have it, but something tells me that I should. I think this baby

has something it needs to do here, and I think it
needs me to help it on its way. Maybe that's stupid.
But I can't stop thinking about that astrologer Sarah
and I went to, the one who told me that I was going
to face a great challenge this year, and that if I ran
away from it I would lose something valuable, but
that if I accepted it it would bring great things into
my life later on. This is definitely a challenge.
I can't imagine a bigger one. Still, I don't know if
this is the right decision. I'm going to think about it
for a few days.

Annie finished the first entry and stopped read-ing. Her mother had gone to an astrologer. *There it is again*, she thought. Why was astrology coming up again and again in her life? She knew from her past experiences that when something kept jumping into her path it usually meant that she was supposed to pay attention to it. Having her chart done had led her to the diary. Maybe there was a reason for that.

She flipped the pages, looking at other entries. Reading it was like reading a story she already knew the beginning and ending to but didn't know the middle of. Each new entry gave her more insight into what her mother had been going through during her pregnancy.

December 7, 1977
Mom called today and asked if I was coming home
for Christmas. I said I would, even though I'm really

*scared. What if someone notices that I've put on
weight? I can hide it under sweaters, but it feels so
awful having to keep this from them. But I know
they just wouldn't understand. Dad would be so
disappointed, and Mom would want me to keep the
baby. I wish they could be like Peter's family. They've
been so good to me. I know Mom and Dad love me,
too, but it's just not the same. I always feel like I'm
doing the wrong thing when it comes to them.
When I have children, I want to be sure they know
that—whatever they do—I'm proud of them.*

Annie skipped ahead, wanting to read what her
mother had written during the final days of her
pregnancy. She found an entry dated May 3, 1978.

*I know it's going to be any day now. I called the
caseworker at the adoption center this afternoon
and told her to alert the adoptive parents. When I
hung up I cried for about an hour. I know I'm doing
the right thing—that we are doing the right thing—
but it still hurts. I keep telling myself that when the
time is right I'll have more babies, ones I'm ready
to care for. Someday I'll hold a daughter or son in
my arms and sing to her or him. I know I will,
just like I know that this baby will be going to a
family that loves it just as much as I do. I wonder
if this baby will ever meet me and Peter, or our
children. I don't see how, but you never know. If that
happens, I hope he or she knows that I did this*

because I loved him or her. I hope so more than any-
thing.

That was the last entry in the journal. Annie didn't know what day her mother had given birth on, but she figured it must have been shortly after that. Then she must have put the journal away, or maybe even forgotten about it. But somehow it had found its way to Annie, and she was happy that it had.

The last entry stayed in her mind. What if she could meet the baby her mother had given up? What would she say? Would she give her the journal so that she could know what their mother had been thinking while she was pregnant?

It's not like I'll ever get the chance, she told herself. She wouldn't even know where to start looking for the woman. But at least she had the journal and the pictures. They helped her piece together part of the story, and maybe that was enough.

She began to put the journal back into the box. She would read it later. But as she did, something slipped out and fell to the bed. Annie picked it up. It was a piece of paper, yellowed with age. Annie unfolded it.

It was a letter. Annie scanned it. It was from the adoption agency her parents had gone through, and it was a form letter stating that they were giving up their rights to their baby. Her parents' signatures were at the bottom. And at the top was the name, address, and phone number of the adoption agency. Annie stared at it for a moment as a thought came to her.

I wonder, she thought suddenly. She looked at the agency information again. It had been a long time ago. *And probably they wouldn't tell you anything anyway*, she argued with herself. But the more she thought about it, the more the idea took hold of her. Finally she sighed. "It's worth a shot," she said, making up her mind.

CHAPTER 15

"I haven't been here in a long time," Kate said, looking around the coffee shop. "It looks pretty much the same."

"I think it's looked like this for the past thirty years," Tyler commented. He was folding a napkin in half and then in half again.

"Are you trying to do origami or something?" asked Kate.

"Excuse me?" said Tyler.

"Your napkin," Kate said, nodding at the now-mangled piece of paper.

"Oh," said Tyler. "No, I was just trying to . . . I mean, the best I could do would be a paper airplane, and I don't think it would get that far. I spilled some water on this."

Tyler was clearly nervous. *But not as nervous as I am,* Kate thought to herself. She still couldn't quite believe that she had agreed to meet him at the restaurant. She'd been so shocked to hear his voice when he called that afternoon that she'd agreed to see him before she realized what she was doing. Now she was sitting across from him in a booth, trying to think of something to talk about.

"Thanks again for the picture," she said finally.

Tyler nodded. He'd barely said five sentences since she'd arrived, and she wondered what he was thinking. *After all*, she thought, *he was the one who asked* me *to meet him.* It seemed to her that it was up to him to keep the conversation going.

"So, how are the girls?" he asked finally.

"Good," said Kate, relieved to have something to break the silence. "Well, maybe not so great. Cooper is having a tough time. Her mother is kind of losing it a little because of the divorce."

"Sounds rough," replied Tyler, although he hadn't really seemed to hear what Kate was saying.

"And Annie's aunt is getting married," Kate continued. "That's pretty cool."

Tyler nodded, and once again Kate got the distinct impression that he wasn't paying any attention to her. She decided to find out.

"Oh, and Sasha discovered the fossilized egg of the world's oldest dinosaur in her backyard," she said brightly. "The Smithsonian is going to pay her six million dollars for it and name a new building after her."

"Cool," responded Tyler.

"All right," Kate said. "That's it."

That seemed to get Tyler's attention. His head snapped up and he looked at Kate with a puzzled expression. "What'd I do?" he asked.

"You asked me to meet you here and now you're acting like you want to be anyplace but here and with anyone but me," Kate snapped. "So either start talking or I'm out of here."

Tyler held up his hands. "You're right," he said. "I'm sorry. Maybe this was a mistake."

"I'd tell you," Kate said, "but I don't even know what *this* is. Maybe you can enlighten me."

Tyler sighed. "I thought we could try talking," he said. "But maybe I was wrong."

"Talking only works if both of us talk," said Kate.

"I know," said Tyler. "This is just harder than I thought it would be."

Kate was angry, but she backed off. She saw that Tyler really was having a difficult time being around her, and she knew that giving him a hard time wasn't going to help matters. *Then again*, she thought, *it's not like you really want to talk to him.*

Or was it? Ever since he'd shown up at her birthday party, she'd been thinking about him. How could it be that someone she was once so crazy for could now seem like a complete stranger? What had happened between them that things had gone downhill so fast? When she looked at Tyler now, she felt as if she didn't know him at all.

"I know you're angry at me," he said finally. "And I don't blame you. I'm angry at me, too."

"Not half as much as I am," Kate informed him,

unable to resist the temptation.

"Probably not," agreed Tyler. "But I am angry. And I'm sorry. I don't know what happened, Kate. It was like you and I were this great couple and then all of a sudden you were gone and I was alone."

"I was alone, too," Kate said defensively.

"I'm not using that as an excuse," said Tyler. "I'm just trying to talk about this. Okay?"

He looked at her, his usually shining eyes dark with a combination of fear and irritation. Kate looked away. "Okay," she said.

"What happened with me and Annie was totally out of the blue," Tyler said.

Kate felt her insides beginning to churn. Hearing Tyler say "me and Annie" made her think of them together—of what they'd done together. She didn't want to think about that. It just made her angry.

"When you weren't around me, I thought of all of these reasons why you and I didn't make sense together," Tyler continued. "We're so different."

"You've mentioned that before," Kate said, a chill in her voice. "I get it—we're not compatible."

"That's just it," Tyler said. "I keep thinking that, but then I realize that I miss you."

He stopped speaking and looked anywhere but at Kate. "I miss being with you," he continued. "I miss talking about stuff."

"Didn't you and Annie talk about stuff?" asked Kate, sounding more nasty than she'd intended.

"What do you want me to tell you, Kate?" Tyler asked. "Do you want me to say that I liked being with Annie? Yes, I liked hanging out with her. I liked doing things with her. I liked talking to her."

It was Kate's turn to look away. She didn't want to see Tyler's face when he talked about Annie. She didn't want to see his eyes light up when he said her name, or watch him smile when he thought about being with her.

"Annie is a wonderful person," Tyler continued. "And you know that. She's one of your best friends."

Now's a good time for you to remember that, Kate thought, but kept her mouth shut.

"You're beating yourself up over this," continued Tyler. "You want to think that the thing with Annie happened because I liked her better. Well, it didn't. It happened because we spent a lot of time together while you and I didn't. It happened because I'm not perfect and neither is she. That's the only reason."

That's the problem, Kate thought suddenly. *I thought Tyler was the perfect boyfriend.*

"I'm not asking you to get over it, Kate," said Tyler. "I'm not even asking you to understand it."

"Then what *are* you asking, Tyler?" asked Kate. "Did you just ask me here so you could unload and feel better about everything?"

"I asked you here because I want to see if we can start over," said Tyler.

Kate stared at him. Was he kidding? Start over?

"This is the place where we had our first date," Tyler said. "Do you remember that?"

Kate nodded. Of course she remembered it. She hadn't known it was a date when she'd arrived. In fact, she'd been going out with someone else when she'd walked through the door. Scott Coogan, the former love of her life. But by the time she and Tyler had walked on the beach, and he'd kissed her, she'd known that she and Scott were over. She'd known it as soon as she'd looked into Tyler's golden eyes and realized that she wanted to kiss him back.

"I know we can't go back that far," said Tyler. "Too much has happened. But maybe we can go back a little bit, just to the point where things started to not make sense."

"And then what?" asked Kate.

"We'll have to wait and see," said Tyler.

Kate didn't say anything. She was thinking. After a minute she looked up and said, "Come on." She stood up and pulled on her coat.

"Where are we going?" Tyler asked, scrambling to follow her. "We haven't even ordered anything."

"I'm not hungry," said Kate as she walked toward the front doors.

Tyler followed her as she left the coffee shop and walked along the wharf on which it was located. She headed for the set of long, narrow stairs that led to the beach and walked down them with Tyler behind her, not saying a word. When she reached the sand she kept walking until they came to the enormous rock that jutted out from the beach into the ocean. A set of smaller rocks, like natural steps, led to the top of it. Kate climbed them and stood on top of the big rock. Tyler climbed up after her.

"Why did you want to come out here?" he asked.

The wind was blowing Kate's hair. She pushed it out of her eyes and looked around. The sea was choppy because of the weather, and the air was thick with mist that chilled her skin. High above them, though, the sky was clear and black. Kate looked up at the stars.

"A lot of the important decisions I've made in my life have been made on this rock," she told Tyler. "I don't know why. Maybe it's because I feel safe up here, like nothing can get to me and I can think about things in peace. Maybe it's because I feel close to the Goddess here, next to the ocean." She looked up at the sky. "Or maybe it's because those stars have something to do with the decisions I make," she added. "We've been talking a lot about astrology in class lately. I'm not sure whether or not I believe that the choices we make are controlled by what's up there or not, but I do know that this place is important to me."

Tyler stood on the rock, his hands in his pockets, and looked at Kate. He seemed to be waiting for her to make a choice. She looked away from him and stared out at the ocean. How many times had she done the same thing, trying to decide what the right thing to do was? How many times had she stared off into the distance, where the waves and the sky met in a thin line of gray, and waited for an answer to come to her? The moments flashed in front of her: kissing Scott and then, later, throwing the ring he'd given her into the waves; kissing Tyler; confronting him and Annie. One after another they came into view, like a collage of images from her life.

Suddenly she realized something: every time she'd come to the rock it was because she wanted a guy to like her, or because she felt bad about what a guy had done to her. It was never about feeling good about *herself* or about what she was doing with her life. It was always about someone else.

Her eyes moved to the little cove beyond the line of rocks. In that cove she, Annie, and Cooper had done their first real ritual together. There she had felt strong and confident, not needy and anxious. In the cove, lifting her hands to the sky or dipping them into the ocean's waves while working magic, she had been connected to the power of the earth, and to the power within herself. But on the rock she had only felt the temporary thrill of having someone want her.

She looked at Tyler, at his handsome face and beautiful eyes. He looked just as he had the first time she'd come there with him. That night she'd felt like the luckiest girl in the world because he had looked at her the way he was looking at her now. She'd needed someone to look at her like that, to make her feel special.

But tonight she realized that she needed something different. She didn't need to feel special. She *was* special. And she didn't need to be with someone else to feel that way. She felt it every time she meditated, or performed a spiral dance with her friends, or called on the Goddess. She felt it whenever she took another step along the path she'd dedicated herself to.

"Maybe we can go back," she said to Tyler. "But not to where you want to go." She laughed. The anger she'd been feeling toward Tyler—and toward Annie—was gone. She didn't need it anymore.

"Where does that leave us, then?" asked Tyler.

Kate looked at him and smiled. "Friends," she said. "It leaves us as friends. I don't need a boyfriend, Tyler," she explained. "What I need are friends. You were right the first time—you and I are really different. That's what I liked about being with you. It's what I still like. But not as your girlfriend, as your friend."

Tyler lowered his head, looking at his feet. When he looked back at Kate, he had a wistful expression on his face. "Maybe you're right," he said. "Maybe this is how it was supposed to be all along and we just didn't see it."

Kate shrugged. "I'm not complaining," she said. "Are you?"

Tyler gave a lopsided grin. "No," he said. "I guess I'm not."

"So," Kate said. "Friends?"

Tyler nodded. "Friends," he said, extending his hand.

Kate took it and held it tightly for a moment as she looked up at the stars. As she and Tyler watched, a shooting star fell through the heavens.

"Make a wish," Tyler said. "Quick."

"I wish I always felt this good," Kate said.

"Gee, thanks," replied Tyler. "It's always nice when a girl feels good after rejecting you."

"I'm not rejecting you," Kate said, giving his hand a final squeeze and then letting go. "I'm just redefining our relationship."

"Oh," Tyler said. "That makes me feel *much* better."

Kate laughed. "Come on," she said. "I'll make it up to you. I'll buy you a sundae."

She climbed off the rock. Tyler came after her. "Okay," he said, "but if you really want to make it up to me it has to have chocolate sauce *and* peanuts."

CHAPTER 16

"Thanks for inviting me out with you guys," Jane told Cooper as they drove to Cooper's house on Sunday afternoon.

"It's not like you haven't been out with us before," said Cooper, teasing her.

"I know," Jane replied. "But that was before."

"Before what?" said Cooper, knowing what her friend was saying and determined not to let her get away with it.

"Before you all knew," Jane said. "That's all."

The light ahead of them turned yellow, and Cooper brought the car to a stop. She turned to Jane. "You're no different now than you were before," she said.

Jane smiled. "I know," she said. "That's what they say in all of the books that people read when they find out someone they know is gay." She looked at Cooper. "But you know what? I *am* different. This is a part of who I am that you didn't know about before. Now you do. I want to be able to talk about it, and I want you to be able to talk about it if you want to."

"Sure," Cooper said. "That's cool." The light changed and she put the car in gear.

"I know we're all supposed to be enlightened and okay with everything these days," continued Jane. "But it's okay if you're a little freaked, or if Annie or Kate or Sasha is freaked. I don't expect everyone to think that this is the greatest thing that's ever happened to anyone. I mean, I'm still getting used to it, and I certainly don't want you guys being more well-adjusted than I am."

Cooper laughed. "Believe me," she said. "We're *so* not."

She turned onto her street. "I need to stop home before we meet up with everyone," she said. "It will just take a minute."

The truth was, she wanted to check on her mother. Since she and her father had confronted Mrs. Rivers, things had gotten even more tense. Now her mother spent most evenings in her room. When Cooper did see her, her mother barely spoke to her. It was like living with a stranger, and it hurt Cooper to see it happening. But even though she'd tried twice more to talk to her mother, Mrs. Rivers wouldn't discuss what was going on. She was gone before Cooper left in the morning, and when she came home she headed right for her room, usually carrying a glass in one hand and a bottle in the other.

Even though her mother was shutting her out, Cooper still wanted to make sure she was okay. Cooper knew what it felt like to think you were alone with a problem, and she knew that eventually her mother would decide to talk about it. She just needed time. Until then, Cooper was keeping an eye on her.

They reached the house and Cooper parked the car. She hesitated before she got out. Should she ask Jane to come with her? She hadn't told Jane about her mother's recent problems, not wanting to dump on her friend when she was going through her own issues. But she thought it would look weird if she asked Jane to wait in the car. Perhaps, she thought, Jane would mistakenly believe that Cooper was trying to hide her from her mother, instead of the other way around.

"Come on in," she said finally. "I don't think you've ever seen the house, right?"

Jane shook her head. "You've always come to mine," she said, opening her door.

They walked up the path to the front porch. Jane stood there, looking up at the old stone house. "This is amazing," she said.

Cooper sighed. "Welcome to historic Welton House," she said, adopting her best tour guide voice. She often had to show tourists around the historic home her family lived in, and she had the patter memorized. She opened the door and ushered Jane inside. "We will begin our tour in the entry hall. Please do not touch anything or employ flash photography."

Cooper gave a quick glance into the living room to see if her mother was in there. She wasn't. *Good*, Cooper thought. *She's in her room, where Jane won't see her.*

"This place is gorgeous," said Jane, admiring the polished wood and the antique furniture. "I can't believe you actually live here."

"Neither can I sometimes," Cooper replied. "Come on, I'll show you my room."

They started up the stairs, but came to an abrupt stop halfway as Mrs. Rivers appeared at the top. She was wearing the same clothes Cooper had seen her in the night before, and her hair was a mess. Even worse, her makeup had smeared on her lips and eyes, and she looked like she had been crying and rubbing her hands across her cheeks. She looked at Cooper and Jane with unfocused eyes, surveying them as if she had no idea who they were or where she was.

"Hi, Mom," said Cooper, praying that her enthusiastic tone would snap her mother out of her haze so that she would at least appear normal for a few seconds until Cooper could rush Jane past her and into her bedroom, where she planned on making up a really good story about the flu and the effects of cold medication to explain her mother's appearance.

Instead, her mother began coming down the stairs, holding on to the railing and taking heavy steps. She pushed past Cooper and Jane and kept going. Then, almost at the last step, she slipped and fell heavily, crashing onto the stairs and sliding to the bottom like an overgrown child letting herself bump noisily from step to step. At the bottom she slumped against the stairs, not moving.

"Is she okay?" Jane asked Cooper, her face knotted up in an expression of concern.

"No," Cooper said. "She's not."

She went down the stairs and knelt beside her mother. Hooking an arm on her elbow and another around her waist, she attempted to help her up. But her mother pushed her away.

"Leave me alone," she said, her words heavy. "Just leave me alone like everyone else."

"Come on, Mom," Cooper said. "Let's just get you to the couch, okay?"

"I said leave me alone!" her mother snapped, slapping at Cooper's hands as if she was swatting a fly. "I just want to be alone!"

Cooper let go and her mother slumped back down, her head rolling forward as she leaned against the wall. She looked like a rag doll someone had thrown down the stairs, discarded and forgotten. Cooper wanted to hug her, to hold her and tell her that it would all be okay. But her mother didn't want her to do that. Right now, she knew, her mother wasn't thinking about anything except how unhappy she was.

Cooper looked up the steps to where Jane was

watching the scene being played out below her. She had a look of pity on her face, as well as fear. Cooper knew that seeing what was going on must be very difficult for Jane. Cooper walked up the steps to her and sighed.

"I'm sorry about this," she said. "She isn't usually like this. It's the divorce."

"Should we call your father?" Jane asked quietly.

Cooper shook her head. "He's out of town," she said. "He won't be back until Monday night."

"What should we do, then?" asked Jane.

Cooper looked down at her mother. Mrs. Rivers was slowly pulling herself up, using the handrail to steady herself. Once she was up she started for the kitchen, moving like a machine whose wiring had short-circuited but that was determined to make it to its destination.

"We're going to leave," Cooper said. "That's what we're going to do."

She went upstairs and into her room, where she took a bag from her closet and began throwing some clothes into it.

"What are you doing?" asked Jane, watching her from the doorway.

"I can't be here with her when she's like this," said Cooper. "I need to stay somewhere else for a couple of days. Then maybe she'll be ready to talk. But right now she needs to work this out by herself."

"Are you sure she'll be all right?" Jane said.

"No," Cooper answered. "I'm not sure of that at

all. But I have to hope that she will be."

She finished packing her bag and zipped it closed. Then she picked up her guitar, her backpack with her schoolbooks and supplies in it, and the bag. "Let's get out of here," she said to Jane.

They left her room and went downstairs. Mrs. Rivers was in the kitchen, making a lot of noise as she rummaged through the refrigerator.

"I *know* I just bought more orange juice," they heard her say belligerently. "Where is all the orange juice?"

"Are you going to tell her?" Jane asked as Cooper paused at the door.

Cooper shook her head. "I'll call her," she said.

They went outside and Cooper shut the door behind her. She threw her stuff into the Nash's small storage space and then got in and started it up. Giving the house a last, sad look, she pulled away.

"Where are you going to go?" asked Jane as they drove.

"I'm not sure," answered Cooper. "Maybe Annie's house. I just need to be away from there."

Jane was silent. Cooper glanced over at her and saw her looking out the window pensively.

"I know what I'm doing seems like I'm abandoning her," said Cooper.

"Oh, no," said Jane emphatically. "I wasn't thinking that at all. I was thinking how sad she looked. She looked the way I felt when I took those pills, like she wants it all to just go away."

"Do you think she'll do what you—" Cooper began, then stopped.

"Do what I did?" Jane finished. "I think she kind of already is, isn't she? She's trying to make herself disappear. If I'd really wanted to kill myself, I would have done it. But I didn't. I just wanted to not feel anything, if only for a few hours."

"I feel like I'm just leaving her there," Cooper said. "But something tells me that I have to." She paused, thinking. "One thing this year of studying Wicca has shown me is that sometimes being responsible means taking care of yourself first, and sometimes helping people means letting them fall down."

She thought about Kate and Annie, and the failed spell that had brought them together. They had all learned a lot from that experience, even though it was often painful. And she had learned even more from her ordeal in the woods on Midsummer Eve and her subsequent temporary abandonment of witchcraft. Maybe, she told herself, what her mother was going through right now was similar.

"If it helps any, I think you're doing the right thing," Jane said after a while.

Cooper looked over at her. "Thanks," she said. "It does help."

They arrived at the restaurant where the girls had decided to have dinner out, a Japanese place that Annie had suggested. Cooper parked and she and Jane went inside. They found the other girls gathered around a low wooden table in the corner, seated on cushions on the floor.

"Hey there," Annie said when she saw them. "Sit down. We thought it would be fun to do this the traditional way."

Jane sat next to Sasha, while Cooper squeezed in beside Kate. The others were picking at a plate of something with their chopsticks. Cooper peered at the contents of the plate curiously.

"What is it?" she asked.

"Octopus," Kate informed her, popping a piece of the squiggly stuff into her mouth. "Try it. It's different."

Cooper picked up her chopsticks and deftly pinched a piece of octopus between the ends. Before she could really think about it too much, she put it in her mouth and chewed. To her surprise, it was good.

"Not bad," she said. "Jane? Are you going to try it?"

Jane eyed the octopus doubtfully. "I think I prefer my food without suckers on it," she said, making the rest of them laugh.

"We decided that we're going to try something new once a month," Annie explained to Jane. "This month it's sushi. I mean, we've all had sushi, but not all the different kinds of sushi. So tonight we're experimenting."

"In that case," Jane said, poking at the dish, "I

can't be the only one not trying it." She managed to wedge a piece of the octopus between her two chopsticks and dragged it to her mouth. She dropped it in and chewed, the others watching her face. When she finally swallowed, they all clapped.

"Now can I order something without suckers?" Jane asked hopefully.

Annie handed her a list of the different kinds of sushi. "You can pick anything you want," she said. "As long as it's raw."

As Jane and Cooper looked over the menu, the others chatted. "So," Sasha said, "has anything exciting happened to anyone this week?"

Kate and Annie looked at each other, then at the others. Suddenly they each seemed fascinated by the pink slivers of pickled ginger that sat on the plate of octopus. They pushed it around, picking up pieces and then putting them back down.

"No," Annie said. "Nothing exciting."

"Nope," added Kate. "Nothing here, either."

Cooper couldn't help but notice that her friends were acting suspicious, as if they were hiding something from the rest of the group. She looked from one to the other, trying to read the expressions on their faces. But both of them had on their best poker faces, and Cooper couldn't get any clues from looking at them. Still, she had a pretty good idea that they weren't exactly telling the truth. *Whatever it is*, she thought, *they want to keep it to themselves for now*. She knew that they would tell her when they were ready, and she could wait. Besides, it was time to tell them her own news.

"I left home today," she said dramatically. She enjoyed the startled expressions on her friends' faces for a moment before adding, "Not for good or anything."

She then proceeded to tell them the whole story about her mother and her drinking. When she was done she said, "So I think it's a good idea if I stay away for a couple of days." She looked around the table. "I don't suppose I can shack up with any of you, can I?" she asked.

"Kyle went back to school," Kate said. "You could stay at my house if you want to. I'm sure my parents would be okay with it."

"And you can always stay with us," said Annie.

"I know Thea wouldn't mind at all," added Sasha. "And we have an extra room."

"Hmm," Cooper said. "Decisions, decisions." She was joking, but it really did feel good to know that she had such good friends to help her out when she needed it.

"Why don't you do it by lottery?" suggested Jane. "You can each pick a number between one and twenty. Then Cooper will write a number down. Whoever is closest to her number wins."

"I like it," Kate said. "Cooper is a prize."

"As if you didn't already know that," scoffed Cooper.

"Okay," said Jane. She handed Cooper a pencil

and a sheet of paper from the little pile of sushi order forms that sat on the table. "Write down a number."

Cooper thought for a moment and then jotted her number down. She folded the paper in half and handed it to Jane.

"Now you three each pick a number," Jane told the other girls. "We'll start with Kate."

"Seven," Kate said.

"Nineteen," Annie declared.

"And I'll take thirteen," said Sasha when it was her turn.

Jane opened the paper Cooper had given her. "Fifteen," she read. "Sasha is the winner."

"Who says thirteen isn't a lucky number?" crowed Sasha triumphantly. "I win."

"Congratulations," said Jane. "You've just won yourself your very own houseguest. As for the rest of you, we have this lovely octopus as a consolation prize."

"I think I'd rather have Rice-A-Roni," Kate joked as the waitress arrived to take their orders and found the girls all laughing so loudly that they couldn't even begin to tell her what they wanted.

CHAPTER 17

Annie picked up the phone for the sixth time. She held it in her hand, looking from it to the letter sitting on her lap. She'd been doing it ever since she'd gotten home from school that afternoon. It was Monday, and Aunt Sarah and Meg were out doing some shopping. Annie had the house to herself. Feeling a little bit guilty about it, she was glad that Cooper was staying with Thea and Sasha. She wouldn't be able to keep her secret much longer if Cooper was around. Her friend had a way of finding out *everything*. It had been hard enough not telling the other girls about her missing sister. She knew she *would* tell them, she just didn't know when.

Right now she was trying to make up her mind about calling the adoption agency. She kept reading the letter she'd found, hoping it would help her decide. "Loving Arms Adoption Center," she read, trying out how it sounded. "Call us at 555-298-1547." They were just numbers, but when she read them out loud Annie felt almost as if she were doing a spell. Those numbers might hold the key to unlocking a great mystery in her life. But could she dial them? Could she actually talk to someone on the other end of the line and explain that she was looking for a baby her mother had given up more than twenty years earlier?

"There's only one way to find out," she told herself, and dialed.

The phone rang. Once. Twice. Three times. Annie heard the sound of someone picking up. She almost hung up, but then she heard the unmistakable sound of the telephone company's recorded message—three atonal beeps followed by a dull mechanical voice intoning, "You have reached a number that has been disconnected or is not in service. Please check the number and try your call again."

She listened to the voice repeat the message two more times before she hung up. Part of her felt relieved, but another part felt intensely sad. The one lead she had had turned out to be a dead end. The adoption center had gone out of business. She put the phone back and sat on her bed, staring at the letter.

"I guess I'll never know who you are now," she said, thinking of the baby her mother had given up. And suddenly she was overcome with emotion. She started to cry. Something inside of her wanted more than anything else to know the sister she'd just discovered she had. It wasn't fair that she should find out about her, only to have her snatched away again. There had to be a reason that she'd found out about the baby. But what was it?

She looked around her room and her gaze settled on the painting her mother had done that hung on the wall across from her bed. It depicted Annie as a baby, being held by her mother as the two of them looked out at a moon with a woman's face. Looking at it always made Annie feel better about whatever it was that was bothering her. This time, though, it made her even sadder. Her mother had never gotten the chance to hold her sister that way. She'd had to give her to someone else, someone who might not have held her up to look at the moon as it shone down on them with the face of the Goddess.

The moon in the picture had always seemed very protective to Annie. Looking at it, it reminded her that the Goddess was always out there, looking out for her, ready to help her if she needed it. All she had to do was ask.

That's it, she thought. *I'll ask for help*.

Still holding the letter, she went over to her altar and knelt in front of it. She lit the white candle that sat in the center of the altar. It cast a small ring of light around the Goddess statue that occupied the front part of the little table Annie had covered with a blue cloth and arranged her magical items on.

Annie closed her eyes and imagined herself in the ring of trees she often visited in her private meditations. She imagined herself sitting there, surrounded by the circle of towering trees. Overhead a bright moon looked down, bathing everything in pure, silver light.

"Mother," Annie said, using her favorite word for the Goddess, "I need some help here." She clutched the letter from the adoption agency in her hand. "I know I found this letter for a reason. I know I found out about my sister for a reason. But I don't know what it is, and I don't know what I'm supposed to do. I'd really appreciate it if you could give me a hint. Just a small one. Nothing too big. I know I'm supposed to work this thing out on my own, whatever it is. But where do I start?"

She paused expectantly, as if she expected to hear a voice come out of nowhere and give her the answer she was searching for. She knew well enough that was probably not going to happen, but she waited anyway, in case she was wrong. She wasn't. There were no voices. No mystical figure appeared to her to tell her what to do. Instead, all she heard was the wind in the branches of the trees that encircled her.

"That isn't helping," she said unhappily.

In her mind she looked up at the sky stretching out over her magical grove. It was clear and black, and the stars twinkled gaily over her head. But instead of thinking that they were beautiful, Annie found herself resenting them. It was stars that had gotten her into this in the first place. "So why don't you guys get me out of it?" she asked angrily. "If you know so much about my life, how come you can't help me figure this out?"

She opened her eyes and stared at the candle on her altar. She was frustrated. Clearly meditation was not the answer. But if that wasn't it, then what was? She had pretty much run out of things to try.

Once again she looked over at the picture on the wall. But this time her eye was drawn down to the desk below it, and particularly to the computer that sat there. Looking at it, she suddenly had an idea.

She got up and went over to her desk. Pulling out the chair, she sat down and clicked the icon that connected her to the Internet. When the program was loaded, she went to a search engine and typed in "adoption agency searches." She hit the search button and waited while the computer hummed for a few seconds. Then the screen flashed a list of the various matches it had come up with. Annie scanned the list, looking for anything that might help her.

She found it at the bottom of the second page. "Northern Star Adoption Searches," she read. "Northern Star is a database of active and inactive adoption agencies throughout the United States. Search our records for information pertaining to yourself or others."

Annie clicked on the link to Northern Star and waited impatiently for it to load. She didn't know if it would be any help to her at all, but somehow it seemed like a good chance. Finally the page loaded, and Annie read more about the agency.

"Northern Star was founded as a nonprofit organization dedicated to maintaining adoption records for the purposes of providing those interested in locating relatives, birth parents, or children placed for adoption with the means of locating one another. We maintain a collection of adoption records from state agencies, as well as private agencies who are part of our program. Our database contains a large number of records from agencies no longer in operation. Click here for a list of agencies whose records we have acquired."

Annie clicked on the link and held her breath. Would Loving Arms Adoption Center be one of the agencies, or had she hit another dead end? Her fingers drummed anxiously on the desk as she waited for the list to appear. When it did, she scrolled down the names until she reached the *L*'s. And there it was: Loving Arms Adoption Agency. A notation beside the name informed Annie that the agency had gone out of business about ten years earlier, but that Northern Star was in possession of all of the company's records for the time it was in operation.

"So far, so good," Annie said. "Now what?"

There was a button on the page to click for information on doing a search for someone through Northern Star. Annie clicked on it and read the instructions that appeared. There was a standard form to fill out, asking for whatever information she had about the adoption in question. That part was easy. She knew her father's name and mother's maiden name, and the approximate date of the birth. She filled that all in.

Then she came to part of the form that asked her to write a statement saying why she wanted to find the person she was looking for. "This information, along with your contact information, will be sent to the person if she or he has also registered with Northern Star," she read. "If she or he wishes to contact you, you will hear from her or him directly."

Annie felt her hopes crash. Not only did *she* have to write something, but she had to hope that her sister had also found the Northern Star website and registered with them. What were the chances of that? She probably didn't even know she *had* a sister out there somewhere. And even if she somehow thought that she might, why would she find the same website? The chances were one in a million.

Annie was about to sign off when she looked up at the picture above her desk again. The Goddess's face looked down at her, and it seemed to say, "You found Kate and Cooper, didn't you?"

"That was different," Annie said out loud. But maybe it wasn't. She really believed that she, Kate, and Cooper had been meant to find one another. And all kinds of things had worked together to bring her aunt and Grayson Dunning together. Now she had been given the information about her missing sister. That couldn't be an accident or a coincidence.

"Okay," she said, sighing. "What have I got to lose?"

She looked at the form on her screen and thought. What was she going to say? If she could talk to her sister, what would she tell her? She thought some more. And then she began typing.

Twenty-three years ago my mother and father had to give a baby up for adoption. That baby was my sister. My other sister. I have a younger sister—Meg. But there's an older sister out there I've never met, and I would really like the chance to get to know her. Maybe she's wondering why our parents gave her up. Maybe she's wondering what our mother and father were like. Maybe she's wondering if she has any other brothers or sisters. I'd like to have the chance to answer all of those questions. And I'd like to ask her what she's like, and what her life has been like. I've always been an older sister. Only recently did I discover that I have an older sister. Meg says that it's really a pain sometimes having an older sister who tells you what to do. I'd like the chance to find out.

She read the letter over several times. Did it sound okay? If she were adopted and received such a letter, would she answer it? The questions tormented her. Finally she just hit the send button on the form and watched the letter to her sister turn into an electronic file.

"Thank you for submitting your request," read the screen that popped up next. "If we have contact information for the person you're looking for, we will forward your letter and your information."

That was it. Annie had sort of thought there would be more to it. After all, finding someone you'd been looking for all your life—or even for a few days, as she had—was such a big deal. But ultimately it was reduced to an electronic message. All she could do now, she supposed, was wait.

But of course she couldn't stop thinking about what she'd done. Would her sister ever read her message? What if she did read it but decided she didn't want to contact Annie? That would be even worse. It was better to think that she would never get it at all.

Eventually she forced herself to mostly forget about it by concentrating on her homework. But that only took an hour. Then she tried working on a new painting, but it just wasn't coming along. She was relieved when she heard her aunt and Meg return and she could go downstairs and lose herself in Meg's recounting of their shopping trip. Annie dutifully approved each of the purchases Meg had made—which included some new clothes and, as a reward for putting up with trying on shoes, several books. Then she helped her aunt make dinner. By the time they'd eaten and she'd done the dishes, she had only a few hours to kill before she could go to bed. She passed the time practicing her Tarot card skills and writing in her magical journal.

Fortunately, the next night she had class to occupy her. Unfortunately, Olivia Sorensen was still teaching them about astrology, and they spent the evening talking about transits and eclipses and other things that Annie jotted down in her notes and tried to understand, but wasn't sure she really understood at all. Thinking about stars made her think of Northern Star, so she concentrated instead on memorizing what astrological signs went with what birth dates. But she kept getting Sagittarius and Capricorn mixed up, and eventually it all became a gigantic blur.

She was relieved when it was time to go home. She was even more relieved when Sophia announced that, starting the next week, they would be moving on to another topic. Astrology was beginning to get on Annie's nerves big time, and she was happy to leave it behind.

Cooper had driven to class, since she was still staying with Thea and Sasha, and she offered to give Annie and Kate a ride home. They all scrunched into the Nash and headed through town.

"Have you talked to your mom?" Kate asked Cooper.

"Yeah," said Cooper, sounding tired. "I told her that I thought she needed some time by herself. She didn't seem to care one way or another. My father wanted me to come stay with him, but I think it's better if I stay with Thea and Sasha. I don't want my mother to think I'm choosing my dad over her."

"When do you think you'll go home?" asked Annie. She couldn't imagine being away from her family like that, even for a night, and she wondered how Cooper was handling it.

"I honestly don't know," said Cooper. "Thea says I can stay as long as I need to, but I don't want to be there for too long. It feels weird going to my house to get stuff and then leaving again."

"You know you're welcome at our house any time," Kate told her.

"Same here," added Annie.

"Thanks," Cooper said. "But I hope I can go home soon."

They drove the rest of the way in silence. Cooper dropped Kate off first.

"'Bye," Kate said, leaning in the window after getting out. "Oh, and Annie, I'll call you in a little bit with that chocolate cake recipe I was telling you about in class. You'll love it."

Cooper continued on to Annie's house.

"Have you noticed that Kate's been really perky lately?" Annie asked as they drove.

"How could I not?" Cooper remarked. "Something has happened to that girl. Any idea what it is?"

"None," answered Annie. "But as long as she's through being mad at me, I'm not going to ask."

Cooper stopped outside the Crandall house.

"This is you," she said to Annie.

Annie started to get out, then turned to Cooper. "Everything is going to be okay," she said, "with your mom. I know it sounds stupid, but I just think it will."

Cooper smiled at her. "I think you're right," she said. "I just hope it happens soon. Don't tell anyone I said this, but Thea is the *worst* cook."

Annie laughed. "Good night," she said, waving good-bye to Cooper as she pulled away.

She walked into the house just in time to hear her aunt say, "Oh, wait a second. Here she is." Aunt Sarah held up the phone. "It's for you," she said.

Kate didn't waste any time, Annie thought as she took the phone and walked into the kitchen.

"Hey," she said. "Let me get something to write with and you can give me the recipe."

"Recipe?" said a strange voice.

"Oh," Annie said, surprised. "I'm sorry. I thought you were Kate."

"No," said the woman on the other end, laughing warmly. "My name is Juliet Garrison." She paused. When she spoke again, her voice trembled with emotion. "I think I might be your sister."

follow the

circle of three

with book 13:
and it harm none

The broken glass that littered the floor was not the worst of it. That could be swept away—was, in fact, being swept away by Archer when the girls arrived at Crones' Circle the next morning for the workshop. Already most of it was in a pile, ready to be thrown into the waiting trash can.

"What happened?" Annie asked as she, Cooper, and Kate stood in the open doorway, looking around.

The store was a mess. Books had been thrown onto the floor. Shelves had been ransacked. Candles of all colors were scattered on the floor, and the jars of incense had been overturned, their multi-colored powders blending together in a fragrant stain. Sophia stood by the cash register, looking at smashed cases that had once held jewelry—pentacles and Goddess pendants and silver rings—and at the open cash drawer in which nothing but a few loose coins remained.

"Somebody broke in last night," she said.

The girls entered the store, stepping over the broken glass and the spilled incense. Simeon, the big gray cat who called Crones' Circle his home, came out from beneath a bookcase and began rubbing against Cooper's leg.

"At least they didn't hurt Simi," said Sophia.

"Do you have any idea who did this?" asked Kate.

Sophia shook her head. "No," she said unhappily. "We left here at around ten o'clock last night and everything was fine. When Archer came in this morning to set up for the workshop, this is what she found."

"What about the alarm?" Cooper asked. "Why didn't it go off?"

"We're having a new one installed," answered Sophia. "The old one wasn't working." She surveyed her store, taking in the mess. "At least no one was hurt," she said, obviously trying to make the best of a bad situation. "That's the important thing."

"Hey, what's going on?"

The girls turned to see Sasha coming in. She was carrying a cup of coffee from the shop around the corner, and she was wearing sunglasses. When she saw the condition of the store she removed her glasses and let out a low whistle. "It must have been *some* party," she said.

"We'll help you clean up," said Annie to Sophia.

The girls all pitched in, returning books to the shelves, straightening up what could be straightened, and throwing out what couldn't be salvaged. Within a short time the store looked a lot better, but it was still a bruised and battered version of its old self.

"It looks like they only took what they thought they could sell," remarked Cooper as they worked. "There are no books missing, just stuff like jewelry and cash."

"Whoever did it must have known the alarm wasn't working," Archer said. "No one would try to break into a store with an alarm system. They'd have to be nuts."

"Who knew about the alarm?" asked Annie.

"Just the repair guy and everyone who works here," answered Archer.

"That's a pretty short list," Cooper said. "Why would any of those people want to steal from the store?"

"That's what makes this so weird," remarked Sophia. "No one who works here *would* steal from the store. We all own it together. If someone steals, she's really only stealing from herself."

"Maybe someone was watching the place and noticed that you weren't setting an alarm when you left at night," suggested Sasha as she restacked a table of books.

"Maybe," Sophia said. "It doesn't really matter,

though. What's done is done. All we can do is go forward."

"You have insurance though, right?" asked Sasha. "I mean, this is all covered?"

Sophia shook her head. "Our policy doesn't cover theft," she said. "We save money by having a very basic policy. So this all comes out of our pockets."

Sasha frowned. "Oh," she said quietly, and went back to cleaning up.

"I just can't believe someone would do something like this," Kate said. "It makes me so angry. I wish we could do a spell or something to teach the person a lesson."

Archer put an arm around Kate as she walked past carrying the broom. "Didn't you learn *your* lesson about putting spells on people the hard way?" she joked.

Kate blushed. "You know what I mean," she said. "I just hate to see whoever did this get away with it."

"You never really get away with anything," said Sophia. "Remember what the Law of Three says: whatever energy you put out comes back to you three times as strong. I imagine that whoever broke into the store is really hurting." She looked around the store. "But that doesn't mean I wouldn't like to tell that person a thing or two."